Ivy's Inheritance

By Linda Shenton

Matchett

Ivy's Inheritance
By Linda Shenton Matchett

Copyright 2025 by Linda Shenton Matchett. All rights reserved.
Cover Design by: Wes Matchett
Photo Credits:
Woman: Shutterstock/Elena Preo

ISBN: 979-8-9877458-8-5

Published by Shortwave Press

Without limiting the rights under copyright reserved above, no part of this publication may be reproduced, stored in or introduced into a retrieval system, or transmitted, in any form, or by any means (electronic, mechanical, photocopying, recording, or otherwise), without the prior written permission of both the copyright owner and the above publisher of this book.

The scanning, uploading, and distribution of this book via the Internet or via any other means without the permission of the publisher is illegal and punishable by law. Please purchase only authorized electronic editions, and do not participate in or encourage electronic piracy of copyrighted materials. Your support of the author's rights is appreciated.

This is a work of fiction. Names, characters, places, and incidents either are the products of the author's imagination or are used fictitiously. Any resemblance to actual events or persons, living or dead, is entirely coincidental.

Drexel Hill, Pennsylvania, 1878

Chapter One

Perspiration trickled down Ivy Cregg's spine as she marched through the corridor toward her father's study, but the moisture had nothing to do with the heat and humidity that had blanketed Philadelphia and the surrounding towns since June. Being beckoned into the opulent room that reeked of cigar smoke never boded well, and the look in Mr. Utterback's eye when he'd delivered the message confirmed her suspicions. What had the butler heard?

She knew better than to quiz the man. Older than Methuselah, his loyalty to her father ran deep and did not extend to the rest of the family, even Mama when she was alive. Her mother's image floated into Ivy's mind, and her steps stuttered. Her hand flew out to steady herself, then she raised her chin and squared her shoulders before continuing down the hallway. She would make Mama proud. No sniveling. No complaining. She'd handle whatever Papa had planned.

He'd changed in the ten years since Mama had been gone. So much that her brother, Waylen, had disappeared into the night after an especially heated argument with Papa two years later and hadn't been heard from since. Ivy's heart clenched. Why hadn't he at least kept in touch with her? Did he think she'd divulge his location? With the five-year age difference, they'd not been close, but did he have no feelings at all for her? What would he think of her now all grown up and acting as Papa's hostess?

Arriving in front of the closed door, she took a deep breath, smoothed her skirts, and patted her hair. She forced a smile, then knocked once and opened the door.

Seated behind the desk and wreathed in a gray cloud of cigar smoke, Marshall Cregg looked every bit the successful and daunting businessman he was. He'd come to America from Ireland as a seven-year-old with his parents, and they had perished on the voyage. Alone, he lived on the streets, absorbed into one of the many gangs of ruffians. An adept pickpocket, he set aside a portion of the coins he stole. When he was old enough to work the mines, he did the same thing with his salary. Success at poker and other card games added to his stash until he finally had enough to purchase the mine.

She'd never learned how he continued to add to his coffers, but she'd heard enough whispers to know he'd left several men in his wake, to say nothing of the workers killed over the years because he couldn't bother adhering to safety measures in his mines.

His charcoal-colored jacket was tailor-made and fit his hulking build like a glove. The white silk cravat at his neck contrasted with his jet-black hair, tanned face, and icy blue stare as his eyes narrowed. His mouth was set in a slash. "I sent for you twenty minutes ago. You know better than to keep me waiting." He motioned to one of the hunter-green upholstered chairs near the desk. "Sit." His voice rumbled in his chest, a voice that caused most men to quake at the sound.

Against her better judgment, she strolled rather than hurried across the room and dropped into the chair. Whatever he had to say must be serious. Normally, he barked his instructions at her while she stood at attention.

She crossed her ankles, then laced her trembling fingers. "Yes, Papa?"

"You're to be married next Saturday."

"What?" Ivy leapt from the chair, then she leaned on the desk when her knees threatened to give way. Her mouth dried, and she licked her lips. "You can't do this."

"I can, and I have." His eyes glittered, and he waved her back into the chair. "You're twenty-five years old. It's about time you had a husband. I've coddled you too much."

"Coddled? Hardly." She barked a harsh laugh. "You're never here, and when you are, you barely give me the time of day. You and your colleagues spend hours behind closed doors, doing who knows what, then you parade me out at your convenience." A chill swept over her, and she lowered herself onto the chair. "Who is the lucky groom?"

"Gareth Heisel."

"No." Nausea threatened to overwhelm her, and she swallowed. Heart threatening to jump from her chest, she glared at her father. "I will not marry that man. He's twice my age and a womanizer, to say nothing of his ruthlessness. You would wed your only daughter to someone like that?"

His face darkened. "Show some respect, young lady. You will do as you're told."

Ivy crossed her arms. "I will not marry the man, and that's final."

Her father rose and strode from around the desk to tower over her. He often used that tactic with others, causing them to cower under his imposing form. She refused to cringe as he barked, "At twenty-five, you are too old for anyone to want, and this may be your last chance for a husband." His gaze clouded for a split second. "Besides, I made a deal, and I'm a man of my word. You will marry the man, and I'll lock you in your room until the blessed event if necessary."

Time. She needed time. With a performance that would make a stage actress proud, Ivy forced a look of submission on her face as she patted her father's arm. "I'm sorry, Papa. I didn't mean to be obstinate. I'll do as you ask, and marry Mr. Heisel, but a woman only gets married once. Is it possible to give me a couple of months to prepare the ceremony and reception? Surely, you want an event that is appropriate for a man of your stature."

He stared at her long and hard, one eyebrow raised almost to his hairline. Would he believe her subterfuge? He was no fool, and smarter men than her hadn't pulled the wool over his eyes. Finally, when she could no longer stand it, he gave her a curt nod, then perched on the edge of his desk. "Very well, the wedding can be put off, but only for three weeks. You're a clever girl; that's more than enough time."

As Ivy opened her mouth to respond, a knock sounded.

"Come!"

The door opened, and Utterback shuffled into the room. "Miss Eastbrook to see you, miss. She's in the blue parlor."

"Thank you, Utterback." Her father waved his hand in a dismissive gesture. "We're finished. I will not be here for dinner this evening, but we will be hosting your prospective groom tomorrow."

"Yes, Papa." She rose and walked from the room, her pulse racing. Alma's appearance couldn't have come at a more opportune moment. Ivy's skirts rustled as she increased her pace. The sooner she broke the news to her friend, the sooner they could devise a plan to prevent the *blessed* event. She burst into the parlor. "Alma!"

Tall and blonde, Alma Eastbrook was every inch the socialite. She'd been born into money and had married well. Despite its simple lines, her lavender day dress probably cost more than Ivy's entire wardrobe. Her hair was pinned up in the latest style with sparkling combs holding her curls in place. Her blue eyes flashed as she jumped up from the sofa. "Is it true? Are you marrying Gareth Heisel?"

Ivy gaped at her friend. "How did you know? Papa only just informed me."

Alma pressed a fist against her chest. "Oh, Ivy, how awful. Did your father own up to the reason? Rumor has it he staked you in a poker game and lost."

"What?" Ivy nearly swooned and grabbed the back of the sofa to keep from pitching forward. "A poker game? I know Papa has been gambling more than usual these last few months, but to bet me? No, that can't be possible."

Looping her arm through Ivy's, Alma guided her to a seat on the overstuffed couch. "There's more. Word is that he staked the mine, too. He's lost everything."

"No." Ivy blinked, and she stared at her friend as she replayed the conversation with Papa in her head. He indicated he'd made a deal. What sort of man tossed his daughter's life onto the poker table?

"Are you going to go through with it?" A deep V was etched into Alma's forehead. "When is the wedding?"

"Never." Ivy sat upright. She would not wilt under this circumstance, and she certainly would not marry Mr. Heisel. "Papa has given me three weeks to plan the wedding, which is hopefully enough time to plan my escape. I cannot remain and become the wife of such a despicable man." She raised her gaze to Alma's. "But where can I go? It would have to be far away. Somewhere neither Papa nor Mr. Heisel can find me."

Alma beamed and snapped her fingers. "I may have the answer you're looking for. I overheard two women at the mercantile talking about a young lady who is leaving town to go to Wyoming as a mail-order bride. She used a matrimonial agency run by a widow out of Boston. Her name is Milly Crenshaw, and she's apparently placed hundreds of girls. You could tell your father you need to travel to Boston to find the perfect wedding gown, and we could talk to Mrs. Crenshaw."

"But I don't want to get married."

"Is it that you don't want to get married, or you don't want to marry Mr. Heisel? Mrs. Crenshaw would pair you with an upstanding man who will treat you right."

"I could find a position as a governess or a teacher."

"As long as you are single, your father can force you to do whatever he wants. You have no rights. He can drag you back from wherever you go to wed anyone he chooses, including Gareth Heisel. If you're already married, he can't do that."

Ivy's stomach roiled, and she wrapped her arms around her middle. "I don't know. Will women ever have charge over their own destiny?"

Alma enveloped her in a quick hug, then cradled Ivy's hands in hers. "We're taking charge right now. We'll both pray that God leads Mrs. Crenshaw to select the perfect groom for you. Now, go tell your father about Boston, and I'll send a telegram on my way home. It's best if it not come from you. Too many wagging tongues. On second thought, I'll have my maid send the cable. Can't have folks in town thinking I'm in the market for a cowboy."

Peace fell over Ivy like a warm blanket. God, is that You?

Chapter Two

Mouth watering, Slade Pendleton tucked the linen napkin onto his lap and smiled. "Are you trying to butter me up, Dinah? You know beef stew is my favorite."

Dinah Childs, wife of his best friend, Nathan, laughed and shook her head as she ladled the fragrant concoction into his bowl. "I have no motive other than to fill you up with good food. Nothing against Cookie, but why you don't get yourself a housekeeper instead of eating with your ranch hands, is beyond me. Not to be indelicate, but you can afford more staff."

Nathan held up his hand. "Now, honey, Slade doesn't need our interference."

"I'm merely making an observation." Dinah wrinkled her nose as she served her husband. "He works hard and deserves the best." She filled her bowl, then gestured toward the pile of biscuits. "Eat up. You men had a full day of branding. You must be starving."

Slade grabbed three of the golden-brown biscuits and laid them on the small plate near his glass. He cracked them open, and steam wafted toward him as he slathered the flaky centers in strawberry jam. "I'm pleased we were able to finish. I thought it would take us a full three days to mark all the new cattle, but we managed to get it done in two."

"Combining our ranches' hands was a brilliant idea." Nathan scooped a spoonful of stew. "Wish I'd have thought of it, and I don't understand the math, but it was more efficient, and that's all that matters."

The trio ate in silence for several minutes, the clink of silverware the only sound in the room. Slade reveled in the warmth and friendship of the couple. They'd reached out to him as soon as he arrived in town six years ago and had stood by him ever since. Dinah had gone out of her way to throw a large celebration last year after he'd proved up his land grant. God had been good to him. Starting with a few head of cattle and a fistful of cash from working the railroads, Slade had slowly built the herd and also used part of his acreage for corn. This year he'd expanded to wheat, and the crop had vastly surpassed his expectations.

As if he could read Slade's mind, Nathan said, "Now that you've tackled beef, corn, and wheat, what's next for the Circle S? You're building quite a spread."

Slade pushed away his empty bowl, then wiped his mouth. "I am pleased with my results, but I don't plan to rush into another crop yet.

Perhaps in another couple of years. I want to ensure the wheat will take hold."

"If this year's fields are any indication, I'd say you're going to do just fine." Nathan rubbed his stomach and beamed at his wife. "Delicious as always, Dinah." He reached over to her and stroked her cheek.

She pinked, then swatted his arm. "Behave, Nathan. We have a guest."

Slade's heart clenched at their obvious love for each other. Dinah was a fine woman, as beautiful on the inside as she was on the outside. She'd asked why he ate with his crew, but he'd never reveal to her the loneliness drove him to the bunkhouse. After a few nights of sitting alone in his huge dining room with nothing but the walls to keep him company, he'd fled to take his meals with the men. He smiled. "Nothing to be embarrassed about, Dinah. Nice to see this rogue treat you like you deserve."

"Hey!" Nathan bolted upright. "I'm right here, you know."

Slade laughed and cuffed his friend on the shoulder. "Just keeping you on your toes, old man. Can't let you get complacent."

Dinah rose and began to clear the soiled dishes from the table. Slade climbed to his feet to lend a hand, but she waved him back into his chair. "Sit. I plan to let you boys do the washing up."

"Mighty kind of you, wife." Nathan chuckled.

"It's the least I can do." She shot him a saucy smile.

Tamping down tentacles of jealousy, Slade shifted in his chair and fiddled with his napkin. Dining with them was a mixed blessing. He enjoyed the fellowship and feeling like part of a family, but their relationship always reminded him of the gaping hole in his life. But at thirty-five had that horse left the barn as he'd heard one of his hands say a couple of days ago. Even after more than fifteen years in America, some of their sayings still tripped him up.

Moments later, she'd cleared the table and returned with a heavily frosted chocolate layer cake. She deftly cut two generous slices for Nathan and him, then a smaller piece for herself. Grinning, he said, "Now I know you've got something up your sleeve. Beef stew and chocolate cake during the same visit." He poked a forkful into his mouth and moaned as flavored exploded on his tongue. He savored the bite, then swallowed. "If you weren't already married, Dinah, I'd snap you up for myself."

Giggling, she shrugged, then took a sip of water. She set down the glass with a thump, then sat back in her chair. "Seeing as you've introduced the topic, I may as well share my idea."

His eyebrows shot up, and his grip tightened on the fork. "Yes?"

"Now, honey, I told you it's none of our business." Nathan shook his head. "Slade doesn't need our meddling in his personal affairs."

"Says you. I disagree." Her gaze slid to Slade. "I only have your best interests at heart."

"Said many a woman with a scheme." Sarcasm coated Slade's words, and he winced. "Sorry, Dinah, that came out a little—"

"Bitter?" She blew out a breath. "I understand, but hear me out. You're a good man with much to offer a wife and children. I'm overstepping, but I want to see you happy. The town is growing, but the number of marriageable women is small, and there are none in our church. You know I'm a mail-order bride. It is possible to find happiness that way."

"You're lucky. It's not always like that."

"True, but as believers, we'll pray God sends you the bride He has planned for you."

Slade laid down his fork. Suddenly, the succulent cake held no appeal. "I appreciate your concern, Dinah. You, too, Nathan, but I'm content."

She frowned. "Contentment isn't happiness."

"Honey—"

"It's okay, Nathan; you both deserve an explanation." He looked deeply into Dinah's eyes. "Thank you for caring enough about me to broach the topic, and to want to see me happy." He rubbed the edge of the plate, then huffed out a sigh. "I advertised for a bride a year after I arrived, and—"

"What?" Nathan bolted upright. "You never told us."

"No, and I'm not sure why. I, um, just didn't." Slade cleared his throat. "Anyway, I exchanged letters with two women, then got serious about one of them. Serious enough that I proposed and sent her funds for her journey. I never heard from her again."

"Oh, Slade, how sad." Dinah pressed her hand against her mouth, and tears welled in her eyes.

His lips twisted. Even after four years, the rejection still stung.

Nathan cocked his head. "You could use an agency like we did. Mrs. Crenshaw who placed Dinah did an extensive background check on both of us."

"That was eight years ago. She's probably no longer in business."

"She is." Dinah wiggled in her chair. "We still correspond. You should send her a telegram and tell her we referred you. That we're friends. Then she won't require you to interview with her. We could also send a telegram."

"I don't know…" Slade picked up his now tepid tea. "I've gotten used to my life. I'm getting a bit long in the tooth to consider marriage."

"Nonsense." She picked up her glass. "Thirty-five is not old, and you are a handsome man. Not as handsome as my Nathan…" She winked. "There's no time like the present, and you have nothing to lose by starting the process. You can always decide it's not for you." She sent Nathan a loving glance, then looked at Slade. "But I don't think you will. Mrs. Crenshaw runs a reputable agency. Will you at least consider praying about the possibility?"

"That I can do." Slade's pulse raced. What had he just agreed to?

Chapter Three

Ivy breathed through her mouth as she pressed her handkerchief against her nose to block the acrid smells of coal and sweat. Her prospective groom had sent enough money for her to ride first class, which was significantly better than second or third, with its upholstered seats, but the seats were close, and most passengers hadn't taken more than a sponge bath since beginning their journey. The trip was blessedly shorter than it would have been a decade ago in a stagecoach: days instead of months, but the end of the journey couldn't come soon enough.

Two weeks had passed since the fateful day Papa dictated her marriage to the awful Mr. Heisel, but Mrs. Crenshaw had come through. Was it serendipitous that the matchmaker was in Philadelphia, or had God intervened personally? Alma had secured an interview the following day, and to Ivy's amazement, and perhaps dismay, the woman indicated she had the perfect mate already. After much discussion, Ivy agreed to head West, to Nebraska of all places, to wed an unknown rancher ten years her senior. A handful of days' worth of telegrams, and the man had also agreed.

With no small amount of deception, she'd managed to smuggle a few of her dresses and underthings out of the house to Alma's, who packed them into a trunk. Unfortunately, Ivy had to leave behind her precious books. Did her groom know how to read? Mrs. Crenshaw indicated he was well-off, rich by many people's standards, but that didn't mean he was literate, did it? Would he be generous enough with his money to allow her to purchase books? Would she be too busy keeping his house and cooking to read? Heaven forbid.

Slade Pendleton.

The name almost sounded like it was from a dime novel. Or should she say penny dreadful since he was English. Mrs. Crenshaw had said he came to America to fight in the Civil War. She'd been twelve when the terrible conflict finally ceased. Why would a man travel across the ocean to take part in a war that was none of his concern? What kind of man was she marrying? The matchmaker had vouched for him, but how much did Mrs. Crenshaw really know about Slade Pendleton?

Fortunately, he'd agreed to a thirty-day trial period and didn't expect her to marry him as soon as she stepped off the train. A sigh slipped out, and her seat mate sent her an inquisitive look. Ivy shrugged and turned her attention out the window. The scenery for the first day and a half had been the typical cityscape as she traveled from Philadelphia to Pittsburgh, then north into Cleveland before heading into Chicago. She'd changed trains twice and would do so once more before reaching her final destination in Nebraska. With any luck her trunk would arrive with her.

Vast stretches of forests and green pastures had replaced the crowded skylines. Periodically, one of the meadows held great numbers of cows. Or were they cattle? What was the difference? Alma teased her about having to learn an entirely new vocabulary. Puffy white clouds scudded across the blue expanse overhead. Ivy wasn't worried about the words. It was the idea of being close to the animals themselves that sent her pulse racing and dried her mouth. She was hardly a shrinking violet, and she could ride a horse, but cows? They looked terrifying even from a distance. Was she making the right decision?

An image of Gareth Heisel's leering face floated into her mind, and her stomach tightened. A wave of nausea swept over her. Ivy swallowed against the bile that threatened to overwhelm her. Whatever she was walking into had to be better than marriage to the despicable man who'd visited nearly every day after her father's announcement.

Cruel and demeaning, Mr. Heisel had alternated between treating her with contempt and trying to have his way with her. Ivy shuddered at the memory of his meaty hands around her waist and his wet lips against hers. She'd managed to break free and slapped him for taking liberties. He'd gripped her arms so tightly he'd left deep bruises that were only now beginning to disappear. His gray eyes glittered as he leaned close and said in a venom-filled voice that he planned to break every bit of spirit she had.

Had her father given up on looking for her? Did he think she was somewhere in the heart of Philadelphia? Would Mr. Heisel turn his brutality on Papa, or did he save that for women? She couldn't worry about Papa. He'd caused his own problems with gambling. Perhaps he'd have to sell the house. The house where she'd lived since birth. Where Mama had died. Tears welled, and she blinked them away. God had given her a way out, and she needed to be grateful.

The locomotive's brakes squealed, and steam wafted past the windows as the train slowed and chugged into a station. Ivy squinted through the grimy, soot-encrusted pane. A sign above the platform that teemed with people proclaimed the name of the town: Des Moines. More city than town and significantly larger than the last three stops. She might be able to find something palatable to eat. Another glance out the window, and a man leaning against the doorway of the building met her eye. A lecherous grin formed on his face, and he tipped his filthy hat.

A shudder slithered up her spine. She gasped and turned away, then bent and dug into the canvas bag Alma had filled with food. Cheese and bread would have to suffice. With men such as the libertine who continued to stare at her, she was not safe exiting the train. Would there ever be a time when women could be independent and on their own without worrying about men accosting them?

A moment passed. Then another. Passengers boarded, and the car filled as she peeked out the window. A sigh escaped. The man had moved on and was no longer visible. Settling against the back of the seat she waited for the train to begin the last leg of its journey. Only a few more hours until she met her prospective groom. Her heart pounded. What had made her agree to marry the man? He was British. She was Irish. The British hated the Irish, and the feeling was mutual. Had Mrs. Crenshaw informed the man of her heritage? If not, would he toss her on the street when he discovered her parentage?

She nibbled her lower lip. Should she disembark in Des Moines? With a population of nearly twenty thousand, the city could provide some sort of job, and Papa would never think to look for her there. She climbed to her feet, then the train lurched forward, and she fell into her seat. An opportunity lost. Dare she remain on the train when it arrived in Lincoln?

Boots clunking on the wood, Slade paced the length of the train station platform. Back and forth. Back and forth. Normally an early riser, he'd awakened while it was still dark, his mind racing with possible scenarios about meeting Miss Cregg. Giving up on sleeping, he'd climbed out of bed, lit the lamp, and wandered through the house to ensure nothing was out of place.

He surveyed the house with a critical eye. His prospective bride came from an affluent family. He'd never been to Philadelphia, but he could imagine her home. Large and well-appointed. Rugs from the best weavers. Expensive furniture, perhaps antiques. China from overseas and silver from the finest metalworker. Gilt-framed art. Sculptures. In other words, nothing like his home.

Despite his wealth, he believed in simplicity. Would she call it stark? Very little adorned his walls or the tops of tables. His possessions were of good quality and well-made; however, if an item was produced locally, he saw no need to pay exorbitant shipping rates just to own Hitchcock chairs or a settee from Paine's of Boston.

"Oof!" Slade looked down at the small boy who'd run into his legs, then wrapped his thin arms around Slade's knees. He'd been so immersed in his thoughts he hadn't seen the child coming. With a grin, the little boy craned his neck to gaze at Slade, blue eyes shining.

"Chip!" A young woman dressed in a powder-blue skirt and white blouse hurried toward them, her face flushed. She raised fearful eyes to Slade. "I am so sorry, mister. My brother, well, he, um—"

Slade ruffled the boy's hair and gave the woman an encouraging smile. "There's no need to apologize. He's not bothering me." Slade looked at the child. "A train station can be a dangerous place, young man. Stay close to your sister."

"Yes, sir." Seemingly unrepentant, the boy released Slade, turned, and grabbed the young woman's hand.

"Thank you, sir." Her face still a light shade of pink, she curtsied, then tugged her brother toward the other end of the platform.

Grinning, Slade watched them walk away, the warmth of the little boy's body quickly dissipating. What would it be like to have a houseful of children? Would Miss Cregg be a good mother? Did she want children?

In the distance, the shriek of a train whistle sounded, and Slade's pulse quickened. His life was about the change in unimaginable ways. Was he prepared? Dinah had teased him last night at dinner, and she'd meant well, but by the end of the night he'd been a bundle of insecurities. Yes, he was rich, but did he have the makings of a good husband? His father had been absent more than he'd been home, and when he was in residence, he was not demonstrative, and their conversations at dinner had been awkward and wooden. Slade couldn't remember a time when Father had hugged or kissed Mother. Did he love her? When Slade had announced his intentions to go to America to fight in the war, Father shook his hand and bade him well. So much different than the ebullient Nathan Childs who pounded Slade on the back, cuffed his shoulder, or made any number of physical gestures, to say nothing of his treatment of Dinah. Surely, there was some behavior in between the two extremes that Miss Cregg would find acceptable.

He yanked out his handkerchief and removed his Stetson, then mopped the perspiration from his face before returning the hat to his head and stuffing the hanky back into his pocket. Crowds had begun to fill the platform, so pacing was no longer an option. Not that it did anything to quell his anxiety, but he'd never been one to remain still for long.

Another whistle from the train, this time closer. He should have accepted Dinah's offer to join him in retrieving Miss Cregg. Now, he'd have to fill an hour of conversation with a woman he'd never met.

Several moments passed, and the black locomotive came into view around the curve. A gray cloud poured from the smokestack, swirling around the behemoth. *Clackety-clack. Clackety-clack.* Metal on metal, the driving wheels squealed, and the brakes shrieked. The platform vibrated under Slade's boots. Hissing filled the air as the train slowed, passenger cars rumbling past, then finally coming to rest. Porters leapt to the ground, then stood guard at the open doorways. At the far end of the train, laborers unloaded trunks, portmanteaux, and carpetbags. Travelers poured onto the platform, and Slade searched the crowds.

There! A lone woman dressed in a bluish-green dress gripped a small satchel, her neck swiveling as she seemed to be looking for someone. Slade swallowed. He surmised she was an inch or two over five feet tall. Lovely, albeit a bit wan. Understandable after her journey.

He marched forward, then at the last minute remembered to swipe his Stetson off his head. Bowing slightly from the waist, he said, "Miss Cregg?"

Her eyes widened, and she nodded.

With a smile, he nodded, then raised his voice to be heard among the chaos. "Excellent. I'm Slade Pendleton. Welcome to Lincoln. I hope the trip wasn't too fatiguing?"

She blinked several times, then followed his lead and said loudly, "No more than expected." She made a vague motion toward the massive pile of luggage. I've brought a small trunk. I hope that won't be an inconvenience."

"Not at all." He shrugged. "Is it marked? I can get you settled into the carriage, then take care of your trunk."

Shaking her head, she pursed her lips bringing to mind one his schoolmasters from decades ago. "I'd like to go with you."

"All right." He plunked his hat on his head, then gestured for her to precede him. "After you."

They threaded their way through the mob until they arrived at the dwindling collection of baggage. At his side, she craned her neck, and Slade placed his hand on the small of her back to guide her around a rather portly man. She flinched at his touch and shot him an icy glare.

He pulled back. "My apologies." He'd grown too used to the casual atmosphere of Nebraska. A gentleman in Philadelphia would never have been so bold, but his gesture hardly called for such a scathing look. What sort of woman was she? A prima donna? A pill? A shrew? Had Mrs. Crenshaw withheld information about Miss Cregg's difficult nature? It was going to be a long drive back to the ranch.

Ivy's Inheritance

Chapter Four

Children's laughter and screams peppered the air as Ivy sat on a blanket, surrounded by ladies from the church, and nibbled on a biscuit. The women chatted as she raised her gaze and searched for Slade. He'd left her with his friend's wife, Dinah, before hurrying away to talk with a cluster of men near the wagons. A week had already passed since her arrival, and she still barely knew the man.

The ride from the station to his home fifteen miles outside of town had been filled with awkward silences and equally awkward conversations. Views from the house were breathtaking, and she'd sat with a cup of coffee on the porch each morning after he headed out with the men he said were called hands, to perform chores. He treated her kindly when they were together, but how he expected them to get acquainted when he spent eight hours a day or more working his ranch was beyond her. Is that what life would be like? An hour or two each day so that at the end of a year they'd have spent less than a month's worth of hours together? She'd had more time with the housekeeper he'd hired on her behalf, and probably to act as chaperone.

"Ivy?"

She blinked, and her face warmed as she turned toward Dinah. "I'm sorry. I was woolgathering."

"Are you feeling all right? You've barely touched the food on your plate." Dinah's forehead was wrinkled, and she cocked her head. "It's beastly hot, so perhaps you're not hungry."

"I'm fine. Really. And this heat is no worse than at home. In fact, the air is much drier here. Anyone who can afford it in Philadelphia takes up residence in the country during the summer to escape the humidity of the city. Others own houses near the ocean."

"I'd forgotten how stifling the cities can be. I'm from Baltimore."

A red-haired woman, whose name escaped Ivy, nodded. "I'm from Boston, and it was awful. You're right about it being drier here, although hot is hot."

"Hopefully, the worst of it is nearly over," Dinah said as she fanned herself. "We'll be looking for some of this warmth come winter."

"How are you settling in, Ivy?" The redhead sent her an encouraging smile. "Even when you want to be here, there's a lot of adjustment."

The tightness in Ivy's chest loosened slightly. These women could relate to her. All had come from East Coast cities to marry a man they'd never met and live on a remote ranch far from town. Fortunately, at thirteen thousand people, Lincoln was large enough to have many of the shops and luxuries she was used to, but it was still a fraction of Philadelphia's size. But if she never got into town, it didn't matter how big it was.

She and Slade had yet to talk about his expectations of her. Mrs. Ridings, the housekeeper, did most of the work, cooking meals and ensuring the house was clean. The laundry was sent out, which left few tasks for Ivy.

"It's taking some getting used to, but not in a bad way." Ivy smiled at the woman. "Nebraska is beautiful. The undulating fields of wheat almost look like ocean waves. And the sky is vast with so many different types of birds." She pinched her nose for a second, then grinned. "But the, um, aromas, are taking a bit to get used to. Very, shall we say, earthy."

"Yes, not the same odors as being in the city, but just as strong." Dinah giggled and poked the redhead. "Grace has never gotten used to the smell. She should have married a mercantile owner or a banker."

"Despite the, ahem, fragrance, I wouldn't change anything." Her face shone. "Kane is the best husband a girl could ask for."

Swallowing a sigh, Ivy forced a smile. Would she ever glow like that when talking about Slade? She'd had no expectations of love when she agreed to marry him. Mrs. Crenshaw had been honest when she'd described him as caring and an integrity-filled man, nothing like the cruel and violent Mr. Heisel. Her marriage, if she went through with it, might not be the loving match Dinah and Nathan had, or Grace and Kane, but she'd be safe, and she couldn't put a price on that. "How long have you been married?"

"Three years."

"Congratulations."

Grace set aside her empty place. "Thank you. Have you and Slade picked a date?" She clapped her hands. "I do love a wedding."

"We, um, no, not yet."

A couple who appeared to be in their mid-forties strolled across the grass and stopped near the blanket. The tall man wore a white Stetson, making him appear even taller as he towered over the diminutive woman. A tin star was pinned to the man's shirt.

"Sheriff Denard, nice to see you," Dinah said.

He lifted his hat for moment and dipped his head at Ivy. "We haven't had a chance to welcome Miss Cregg to town. How are you enjoying our fair city thus far?"

"Much different than what I'm used to, but it's lovely." She squinted up at him. "And you're the sheriff, a big job."

"I have plenty of help. Lots of deputies. In fact, Nathan gives me a hand when I need a posse." He put his arm around the woman with him. "Forgive my manners. This is my wife, Olivia."

"Nice to meet you." Ivy climbed to her feet. "Forgive *my* manners. I love your dress. You'll have to tell me where the best shops are located."

Olivia grasped Ivy's hand. "We can make a day of it. I've heard you're from Philadelphia. You can give me all the news from the East Coast, including what the women are wearing now."

"Join us, Sheriff?" Dinah motioned to the blanket. "There's plenty of room."

The sheriff and his wife exchanged a look, then he helped her sit down before lowering himself beside her. He kept an arm around her as she leaned up against him.

Ivy sat down, then plucked at her skirt. Another mail-order marriage, if she remembered correctly, and obviously in love. Perhaps there was hope that she and Slade would develop feelings for one another. If she stayed. "Have you always been a lawman, Sheriff?"

"Pretty much. I was a Pinkerton before the war, then took advantage of the Homestead Act after the hostilities ended but found that ranching isn't for me. I started out as a deputy, and after the last sheriff retired I took his place."

"It must be dangerous work."

He shrugged. "In some ways, it's better than in the early days when it was a town full of men and saloons, and not much else. Then the brides brought a taste of civilization, and as children were born and families formed… Well, like I said, it's better now. Sadly, we still have prostitutes, but we rarely see violence unless one of the gamblers gets mad about losing his money."

Ivy gritted her teeth. Gamblers. Men like her father who bet more than they had. Taking risks. Ruining families. "Gamblers are despicable. They should be locked away, especially those who take advantage of others, people who can't afford to bet."

Sheriff Denard's eyebrow rose. "That's a mighty strong opinion, Miss Cregg, and I'd say there's a story behind that."

Her face heated. "I, uh—" Fortunately, Slade approached, averting her need to answer.

"Ivy, would you care to dance?" Slade held out his hand. "I apologize for leaving you on your own for so long. Business called."

"Shame on you, Slade." Dinah tsked. "Business at a church picnic. You know better than that."

Ivy allowed him to pull her to her feet. It seemed they both needed saving. "I'd love to." She turned to the group as she slipped her hand in the crook of his elbow. "Please excuse us."

He studied her face. "Are you all right? You seem to be in a hurry to get away. Did someone hurt your feelings?"

"I, um, responded rather strongly when Sheriff Denard talked about the gambling problem in Lincoln."

"That's understandable with your particular situation. Later you can explain—"

"No!" She cleared her throat. "I mean, it's no one's business about what Papa did. It's embarrassing enough that I had to tell Mrs. Crenshaw and then you."

"You've nothing to be embarrassed about. What your father did is about him. Not you. But I'll keep mum." They arrived at the wooden platform that had been laid out as the dance floor where several couples were already shuffling to the music. He put one arm around her waist and took her hand in the other to help her onto the platform. Tingles shot from her fingers to her shoulder, and she trembled at the feel of his hand through the fabric of her dress. How could his touch affect her in such a short time?

Ivy's Inheritance

Chapter Five

Sunshine warmed his back as Slade stood with several of the single men a short distance away from the dance floor. He and Ivy had waltzed through two songs until Sheriff Denard cut in. A look of panic had washed across Ivy's face, and her back had stiffened under Slade's hand. He whispered that she could reject the man's request, but that the lawman was the safest choice other than himself, and she acquiesced. Was her life back East so bad with her father's gambling that she had to fear those on the right side of the law? Was there more to her story than Mrs. Crenshaw had indicated?

He frowned and huffed out a breath. Perhaps he should have the sheriff conduct a more extensive background check than the matchmaker had probably done. Slade had given Ivy a thirty-day grace period, but he might need one to see if she was the woman she claimed.

The music ended, and a smattering of applause filled the air. The fiddler raised his bow. "Thank you, folks. We're gonna take a bit of a break." He nodded to a gray-haired woman who was pointing to a quilt stretched on a wooden frame. "The missus is telling me that it's time for you ladies to join her under the trees to help finish Felicia's wedding quilt. For the men we've got horseshoes, and of course, there's still plenty of food left."

As couples on the floor broke up and wandered in different directions, Olivia Denard hurried to Ivy, then linked arms with her. Their heads close together, they sauntered across the grass to join the quilting bee. Ivy was more animated than he'd ever seen her. She was polite to him, but she always seemed to be holding back. Of course, she'd only been in town for a week, and not all women were as gregarious as Olivia Denard or Dinah Childs.

Slade strolled toward the area where a half-dozen pairs of spikes had been driven into the ground about forty feet apart. Men were already gathering and determining opponents with good-natured ribbing.

Nathan looked up and grinned. "Ah, here's my competitor now."

"In the mood to lose, are you?" Slade clapped his friend on the back. "I'm happy to take you on."

"You seem mighty confident. Care to make a wager on that?"

With an exaggerated expression of shock, Slade widened his eyes. "Betting at a church event? Shame on you, Nathan Childs."

Laughter rumbled in Nathan's chest. "Yep, but I'm not thinking money. Let's make it interesting." He rubbed his jaw. "You lose, you help me paint the outside of the house Dinah's been after me to do. If I lose, I'll do something for you."

"You know I'll help you paint whether I lose or not."

Nathan shrugged. "Perhaps. What say you?"

"Sure, and if you lose, I've got a fence that needs repairing." Slade held out his hand. "Deal?"

"Deal." Nathan shook his hand, then pulled a coin from his pocket. "Heads, you go first."

"You're in a gambling mood." Slade's lips twisted, and his gaze slid to the women hunched over the quilt, chattering like a flock of magpies. How easy it was to be cavalier about wagering with a friend, but a habitual life of betting had sent Ivy fleeing across the country.

"Thinking of your prospective bride's situation? A sad story, but she seems to be settling in. The women have fully embraced her. Even Velma, and she looks at everyone with suspicion."

"Can you blame her? Velma's had a tough life."

Slade forced his gaze away from Ivy and picked up his pair of horseshoes. "Enough philosophizing. The sooner I beat you, the sooner I can grab another plateful of food."

"Or make cow eyes at a certain lady from Pennsylvania."

"Cow eyes," Slade sputtered. "I'm not—"

"Yeah, you are. You constantly search the crowd for her. Apparently, you're beginning to have feelings for her already. That's a good sign. That, and you glower when you see another man eyeing her. Although, you've got nothing to worry about. She's betrothed to you. They have no claim on her." Nathan slipped the coin in his pocket, bent, and retrieved his horseshoes from the ground. "Now, forget flipping. Take your turn, and I wouldn't count on beating me just yet."

"Fine." Slade stepped up, aimed, then tossed the shoe, which landed a foot away from the spike. He growled and rotated his shoulders. "It's been a while since I played."

"Uh-huh. It couldn't possibly be our conversation."

Slade threw his second shoe which landed closer. "Maybe we should warm up before keeping score."

Nathan howled with laughter. "If you insist." He threw his shoes in quick succession, both of which encircled the stake. He smirked. "Guess I'm warmed up."

They walked to the stake and picked up their horseshoes. Slade gripped his horseshoe. "She needs a husband, and anyone will do. We're not betrothed. She's agreed to a thirty-day courtship to see if we're compatible."

"Then you'd best get to wooing her, friend." Nathan motioned to the far stake. "Use some of that British charm. My wife is forever talking about your enticing accent."

"Ivy's Irish. The Irish hate the British." Slade shrugged, then flung the shoe which landed inches from the stake. He grunted with satisfaction and threw the second shoe which landed with a clank on top of the first. "Not without reason, if you ask me. I love my country, but her imperialistic, holier-than-thou attitude doesn't sit well with me. Never did, and it's one of the reasons I crossed the ocean."

"Fine, then channel some of that rugged cowboy charm you've developed." Two more pitches. Two more scores. "And you're a handsome bloke."

Slade chuckled at Nathan's attempt at a Cockney accent, then sobered. "Thanks for the compliment, but no matter how good-looking or charming I am, I'll still be British."

"She knew that before arriving, and she came anyway."

"Desperate times call for desperate measures." Slade cast the shoes which landed around the stake. "Finally!"

As they headed to the other end of the playing field, Nathan nudged Slade's shoulder. "Since when do you back down from a challenge?"

With a chuckle, Slade glanced at the group of quilting women. Where was Ivy? Motion, and a flash of blue near the trees, caught his attention. A challenge, indeed. "Perhaps, now is as good a time as any. A quiet stroll away from prying ears—"

Ivy screamed, then dropped to the ground, writhing.

Heart in his throat, Slade sprinted across the expanse, Nathan on his heels. *Please, God, let her injury be a turned ankle.* Seconds later, he arrived at her side. Taking stock of her white face, and her flailing body, he gritted his teeth. He exchanged a glance with his friend, then pulled up her skirts, exposing a pair of puncture wounds in the stocking above her boot. "Snake bite." His pulse ratcheted even faster as he whipped out his pocketknife.

With lightning-quick motions, Slade sliced the stocking, then cut an X on the skin between the fang marks. Murmuring an apology, he pressed his mouth against he wound and sucked out the venom. He spat out the bitter toxin as he shot frantic prayers toward heaven for God to prevent this precious woman's death. He repeated the actions, grateful Ivy had fainted.

A crowd formed, then he heard the doctor's distinctive gravelly voice, "Coming through, folks. Out of the way, please."

He squatted next to Ivy, lifted her eyelids, took her pulse, then put his hand against her forehead. He shot Slade a curt nod. "Don't suppose you got a look at the culprit."

Slade shook his head as he continued to work on Ivy. Several minutes later, he sat back on his haunches and pulled his handkerchief from his pocket. As he wiped his face, the doctor applied a tourniquet around the leg above the bite, then spread some sort of nasty-smelling poultice on the wound and wrapped it with gauze. "I'll get her to the office and then keep an eye on her." He clapped Slade on the back. "Ya done good, son. She's not out of the woods, but she's got a fighting chance of beatin' this, thanks to your fast response."

Slade's stomach roiled. If she died, it'd be his fault. He'd failed to warn her about the dangers in Nebraska. He didn't deserve a wife.

Ivy's Inheritance

Chapter Six

Eyes feeling as if she'd been in a sandstorm, Ivy blinked then winced as light pierced her brain. Where was she? She closed her eyelids. The mattress on which she lay was thin but soft, and a sheet was draped over her body. Her ankle throbbed. What happened? Her mouth was dry, so she licked her lips, then swallowed. Snippets of memory pushed their way into her head. The church picnic. Dancing with Slade. Quilting with the women. Walking. Then sharp pain.

She gasped. What had caused the pain?

Movement to her right, and she startled. Her eyes flew open. "Who's there?"

Slade came into view. He bent over her, his forehead wrinkled in a deep frown. "You're awake." He stroked the side of her face. "How do you feel?"

How did she feel? Groggy. Thirsty. And her ankle ached.

"Where am I? What happened?" Her voice was raspy, and she coughed.

"Doctor," Slade shouted. "Dr. Yokum, she's awake."

The door opened, and a hefty, white-haired man trundled into the room. He beamed at her, then placed a beefy hand on her forehead. "Your fever is gone, and your color is better. I'd say you're going to be just fine." He turned with an agility she didn't expect from someone his size, then worked the pump at the sink and filled a tin cup with water.

Slade put his arm around her shoulders and helped her into a sitting position. His warmth permeated the fabric of her dress, sending heat to her cheeks. He smelled of soap, leather, and perspiration, not an unpleasant aroma.

The doctor held the cup to her mouth, and she sipped the tepid liquid, its wetness soothing her throat. "Take your time, little lady. You gave us quite a scare."

"I don't remember what happened. I was walking. My ankle. It hurts. Did I stumble and sprain it?"

"No, you were bitten by a snake." Slade's breath tickled her face as he talked. "It's my fault you were hurt. Will you forgive me?"

"A snake?" She shuddered. "I didn't see a snake. Do you have many here?"

With a chuckle, the doctor set the cup on the counter. "Plenty, and unless they're sunnin' on a rock, they like to hide in the weeds. You must have disturbed one, and he let you know he wasn't happy about that."

"I'm sorry. I should have warned you." Slade's eyes were red-rimmed and his face wan under his tan. "It's my fault," he repeated.

"Nonsense." Ivy and the doctor spoke in unison, and she glanced at the physician who nodded.

"But—"

"Listen, young man, any one of us can get bit at any time. Accidents happen, and she wouldn't be alive if it wasn't for you being Johnny-on-the-spot. You're the one that sucked out that venom." The doctor looked at Ivy. "He put propriety aside to get to your wound. Saving you was more important than any silly rule about a man not seeing a bit of leg. He's a hero."

Ivy's face burned even hotter, and she slid her gaze toward Slade who squirmed as if he'd been called into the principal's office for a prank. "You saved me?"

He shrugged. "I did what anyone would have done." He patted her hand. "Are you strong enough to sit up on your own?"

"I think so." She gripped the sides of the bed and straightened her spine. Slade removed his arm and tucked the pillow behind her back. She shivered at the loss of his warmth, and the doctor pulled up the blanket.

"Are you hungry, young lady?" Dr. Yokum peered into her eyes. "You need to keep up your strength if you're to recover completely."

Her stomach lurched, and she grimaced. "Not yet, but some tea would be nice."

He opened the door and bellowed into the hallway, "Nurse, tea and toast for our patient." A faint voice responded in the affirmative, and he closed the door with a bang, then leaned against the counter beaming at her.

Aware of the proximity of the two men in the tiny room, Ivy hunched into herself. Slade had seen her legs. Not only seen her legs, but touched them with his mouth, a horrifying thought. Was life that different from that in the East, and societal expectations no longer applied? Granted, she'd been in dire straits, but couldn't he have waited for the doctor? It was embarrassing enough to have a physician be so intimate, but a man she'd only known a week?

If she remained, would she have to live in fear of more attacks by wildlife? Not only snakes, but perhaps beasts. She'd read about mountain lions. Was Nebraska home to the large cats?

"Slade, turn your back. I need to check Miss Cregg's wound."

His boots clomped on the wooden floor as Slade pivoted, stuffed his hands into his pockets, and marched to the corner where a collection of bottles and boxes sat on a scarred wooden table.

Ivy glanced at him to ensure he couldn't see the doctor's ministrations.

With gentle movements, Dr. Yokum set aside the blanket and moved Ivy's skirt to just above the bandage which he peeled back, then leaned toward her leg and sniffed deeply. He nodded and mumbled to himself as he appeared to study the wound from different angles. "Excellent. I don't see or smell any signs of infection, and the swelling has reduced." He replaced the bandage with a fresh one, then put her skirts in place and tucked the blanket around her. "I believe you are going to make full recovery, young lady. She's decent, Slade."

In two strides Slade returned to her side. Relief smoothed the worry lines she'd seen on his face. "Good news, Doc. We appreciate all you've done for her."

"It's that new poultice I've been using. Heard about if from Bernice Bernleigh, you know, the midwife. She's in tight with some of the Natives, and their knowledge for using local plants is impressive. Unlike some of my colleagues, I'm open to alternatives for healing."

"Natives?" Ivy cocked her head.

Dr. Yokum nodded. "The Indians. I'd love to spend a month with them. Could probably learn all kinds of treatments."

"Aren't they savages?"

"Hardly." Slade frowned. "They are a noble people who have been pushed off their lands by American greed. They've been around a lot longer than we have. Some say thousands of years." He leveled his gaze on her. "I've got a couple working on the ranch. I hope that's not going to be a problem for you."

"N-no," she stuttered. Had she answered too quickly? Could she live on a ranch with Indians? Didn't Slade worry about being scalped in his bed? How little she knew about this man. Or this state barely out of its infancy. Would three weeks be enough to determine if she could spend the rest of her life here…with him? Did she have a choice? Were Papa and Mr. Heisel on her trail? What if she waited too long to wed? Why did life have to be so complicated?

Slade dragged a chair across the room to the cot, the wooden legs screeching against the floor. He winced and sent Ivy an apologetic smile as he sat next to the bed. He laced his fingers to keep from holding her hand as a half-dozen emotions washed over her face. He'd seen her embarrassment when she realized what he'd done to save her. The last thing she probably wanted at this stage of their relationship, if one could call it that, was him touching her. He hadn't earned the right.

He cleared his throat. "I can just sit here if you need to sleep again."

Her cheeks pinked, and she shook her head as she plucked at the blanket. "I've slept enough." She turned to Dr. Yokum. "I'm not feeling too poorly. When may I go home, um, back to the Dinah's?"

"I'd like to keep you one more night for observation." His gaze flicked to Slade. "But I don't anticipate any problems, so Romeo here should get a room at the hotel rather than sitting in that chair all night."

It was Slade's turn to redden, if the heat on his face was any indication. "You sure you're up for an all-nighter at your age, Doc?"

"Touché." Dr. Yokum chuckled. "I guess I deserved that." He capped the bottles and returned them to the cabinets, then wiped down the tabletops. "I'll go check on that tea. You know, if I can walk that far." He grinned at Slade, winked at Ivy, then slipped out the door.

Ivy's hand stilled. "You've known each other a long time."

"Yes. Ever since I rode into town convinced that I knew everything about everything. It didn't take long to figure out I didn't."

"There's a story or two behind that comment." A smile tugged at the corners of her mouth. "And tone of voice. I hear regret, embarrassment, and amusement."

"You're very perceptive." Slade rubbed the back of his neck. "I can see I won't ever be able to get something past you." Her eyes clouded, and he held up his hands. What an idiot. He'd reminded her of her father's subterfuge. "Not that I'd want to. There will be no secrets between us. I can promise you that. You may not always like what I tell you, but it will be the truth, no matter what. I hope you can believe me."

She caught her lower lip in her teeth and lifted one thin shoulder in a delicate shrug as an awkward silence filled the room.

Slade licked his lips. "If you're not too tired—"

The door opened, and a woman of about sixty entered the room, carrying a tray on which a steaming cup of tea sat next to a plate with two pieces of lightly buttered toast. She wore a crisp white apron over a powder-blue dress, and her reddish-brown hair was tucked into a white bonnet. "Well, you look much better than when they brought you in.

You'll be right as rain in no time, especially with this strapping young man to take care of you." She put her burden on the small table next to the bed. "Nibble on that, and if it stays down, I'll bring you some nice chicken-and-vegetable soup later. We've got to put some meat on those bones." She stroked Ivy's hair, then wagged her finger at Slade. "Don't be stayin' too long. She needs her rest."

"Yes, ma'am." Slade squelched the desire to salute. Doc Yokum might own the practice, but his nurse-wife was in charge. She was tougher than most sergeants he'd met in the war. "Yes, ma'am," he repeated.

Mrs. Yokum left the room, and Slade exchanged a glance with Ivy who seemed to be stifling a grin. Her eyes twinkled, and she said, "She doesn't brook any nonsense, does she?"

"Not at all, and she takes her nursing seriously. Doc patches up the patients, but she journeys beside them to ensure a full recovery if at all possible. She's got a heart of gold under that gruff exterior." He motioned toward Ivy's food. "Now, you enjoy your snack while it's still hot, and I'll regale you with my exploits and foibles as a rancher in my early days."

Ivy picked up the cup and took a tentative sip. The lines on her face smoothed out as she sighed. "One of the best cups of tea I've ever had. She's a magician."

"Why her patients tend to recover." Slade chuckled. "With all her pampering, you won't want to leave."

"I can believe it." She cocked her head. "Now, quit stalling. I want to hear these stories. You seem so sure of yourself. Your mistakes weren't that serious, were they?"

Slade shifted on the seat, then brushed unseen lint from his sleeves. "Well, each one could be fixed, but I made enough errors that first year, I nearly went out of business before I started. We had an exceptionally rainy spring, and I thought it'd be easier to keep the cattle close by and not move them around. Turns out they make a mess of the field and need *more* space during inclement weather. Then not once but twice I thought I'd fixed fences properly. Told my hands I didn't need any help. I didn't want them to think I was a greenhorn."

"I take it the fences gave way both times." A dimple danced on her left cheek as she smiled. "How many cattle did you lose?"

He ran his hands through his hair. "Fortunately, the man who owns the next ranch is honest, so I didn't lose any, but several dozen sauntered over to his place. He could have made all kinds of trouble for me, or rebranded them, but he didn't."

"I'm glad it worked out."

"He has been a good friend." Slade nodded. "Helped me out with my next mistake. I wanted to do it all and spread myself too thin. I should have focused on just cattle or just crops but was determined to produce high quality corn and beef. Potatoes, too. You know, the whole meal."

Ivy giggled. "I'm guessing it didn't work out so well."

"Better than it would have if he hadn't pulled together hands from all over town to help bring in the harvest. I didn't sleep much trying to do it all. Ended up quite ill, pneumonia brought on by exhaustion, the doc said." His face was warm, and he knew it meant his cheeks were red. She must think him daft. Why did he decide to share how he'd bumbled things in the beginning? "Anyway, I understand if you're feeling a bit out of place. A city girl come to the country. I was in your shoes. London born and bred, but you're smart. If I can learn, so can you. I'll teach you."

She set down the now empty teacup and dropped her gaze. With jerky motions, she reached for the plate of toast, then seemed to change her mind as she withdrew her hand.

He leaned forward and raised her chin with one finger. "Even if you don't stay."

Her eyes widened. "But—"

"But nothing. If you're going to stay out West, or even if you're not, it will be good for you to have the knowledge. We agreed to thirty days. If nothing comes of it, I respect that. Respect you. Your job right now is focusing on getting better so I can teach you." He forced a smile. In the seven short days since her arrival, she burrowed her way under his skin. Into his heart if he dared think that way. Life would lose its shine if she decided Nebraska or him weren't for her.

Chapter Seven

"There's nothing more I can do for you, Miss Cregg." The next morning Dr. Yokum patted Ivy's shoulder. "You're fit enough to go home. Another few days of rest, and you should be able to resume your responsibilities."

Ivy exchanged a glance with Slade, who looked at her with a mingled expression of relief and an emotion she couldn't read. Did he regret her coming? Did he dread her release? She sent the doctor a tremulous smile. "Thank you, sir."

"Oh, let's have none of that 'sir' nonsense. Doc Yokum is fine. Now, Slade and I will wait outside while my wife helps you freshen up and change your clothes so you can be on your way."

"All right, Doc Yokum." She fiddled with the blanket, suddenly aware she still wore the garment from the picnic two days ago. Had it really only been forty-eight hours? So much had happened in that short span of time. Slade had been nothing but solicitous and had claimed responsibility for her injury, but was he just saying that to be polite? Did her think her foolish for not seeing the snake and getting bitten? What else would she have to learn the hard way?

"Good girl." The doctor opened the door and motioned for Slade to follow him. Their footsteps faded, and a muffled voice called for Mrs. Yokum.

Silence, then the woman appeared on the threshold carrying a sage-green gown and underclothes. "This might be a tad loose on you, but I couldn't resist. With that dark hair, you'll look lovely in this."

"I have my own clothes."

"Of course you do, but you won't want to put on that soiled dress after bathing. At some point, you can return the garment. Or not. Consider it our welcome gift to the community."

"Thank you. You're very kind."

Mrs. Yokum tilted her head and studied Ivy. "It seems you might not have had a lot of kindness in your life. I'm sorry about that, but you're in the right place. Lincoln is full of warm and friendly people, and you've got yourself a good man. Slade can be a little gruff on the exterior, but inside he's got a heart as big as Nebraska."

Tears prickled the backs of Ivy's eyes, and she blinked them away. How long had it been since someone had been truly considerate of her? Nice without any sort of agenda. She shook her head and pulled back the cover as the nurse hung the garment on a hook, then laid the rest of the items on the visitor's chair that Slade had recently vacated. She opened a cabinet and pulled out a large, fluffy towel and a bar of soap. "Hold on, honey. I've got a tub coming that will be filled with nice hot water. Can't having you take a cold spit bath, can we?"

"Well—"

The door opened, and Slade walked in carrying a large tub, the muscles in his arms bunched under the weight. On his heels, the doctor carried two steaming buckets of water. In a flash, the men had set up the container and emptied the pails into it. Two more trips, and the task was complete. Mrs. Yokum shooed them from the room, and Ivy's face heated. She hadn't blushed so much in her life as she had since arriving in Lincoln. She wasn't a simpering girl, but her traitorous body reacted in unexpected ways every time Slade was near.

"Let me help you off that bed, then I imagine you'd like some privacy to enjoy your bath. Take as long as you need." She winked at Ivy. "It builds character in a man if he has to wait for the woman in his life."

Gaping at Mrs. Yokum, Ivy allowed the woman to assist her to the floor. Her ankle twinged slightly. Was the nurse serious or trying to set Ivy at ease? She'd had little experience with men and would think about the comment later. Despite Papa's wealth, and to his irritation, she had refused to use a personal maid and always dressed herself, but Mrs. Yokum's gentle yet clinical ministrations soothed Ivy's erratic pulse. She slipped out of the garment, then caught a whiff of her stale scent. Another blush, and she shook her head. In the days he'd been keeping her company, Slade had never once given an indication she wasn't a fresh as a daisy.

"I'll be right outside, so just give a holler if you need anything." Mrs. Yokum gathered up the discarded dress. "Please don't feel the need to rush. I've just started reading Jules Verne's newest book, *Off on a Comet*, and it's very exciting."

"Yes, ma'am."

Seconds later, the nurse had left the room, and Ivy had shed her underclothes and stepped into the tub. She bit back a moan of delight. No need to make Mrs. Yokum think she was hurting. Far from it. Tension slipped from her muscles as she leaned back against the metal tub. She closed her eyes, and minutes passed as she reveled in the warm water against her skin. Events of the last week crowded into her mind, and the two things that stood out were the acceptance and friendliness of every person she'd met, from the woman at the mercantile to the ladies at church who barely knew her. Would they feel the same way about her if she chose not to marry Slade?

Slade.

Her stomach buzzed like a flock of hummingbirds was inside at the thought of him. Why wouldn't she marry him? Should she tell him on the way to the Childs' that they could wed now if he wished? What if he turned her down? Come to think of it, he'd been the one to suggest the thirty-day wait. Did he need time to determine if she was worthy? To decide if she was what he was looking for in a wife? What was he looking for? Would she measure up? She was hardly prepared to live on the prairie, let alone be his partner in running a ranch. She should tell him she didn't know anything about being a ranch wife. She stifled a laugh. Surely, he was already aware of her lack of skills. Allowing herself to get bitten by a snake was proof enough of that. Her lips twisted. Better to be bitten by a real snake than to marry the one she'd fled in Pennsylvania.

The wagon creaked as it lurched down the lane that led to Nathan and Dinah Childs's home. Slade snuck a peek at Ivy whose wan complexion spoke of her fatigue. At the doctor's he'd offered to fill the back with blankets so she could recline for the journey, but she refused. Did she rue her decision? If she was to remain, that sort of tenacity would serve her well.

She must have felt his stare because she turned to look at him, her gaze seeming to search his face for some sort of answer.

He smiled. "I'm sure you're ready for a lie-down."

"I am tired, but truth be told, I'd like something to eat if it's not too much trouble for Dinah. I'm sure she's busy with ranch work."

"Knowing you're on your way, I doubt that. She'll have a spread ready and will expect to feed you before tucking you into bed. She's a formidable force, so beware."

Giggling, Ivy nodded. "I figured that out early on. Nathan met his match in that one. I understand he was a Pinkerton detective before they met."

"Yes, and it's a wonder they got together. Her brothers were part of a gang that was responsible for the death of his first wife. But Dinah was never involved in their illegal activities and, in fact, left Maryland because she didn't want to be associated with them."

"We have more in common than I thought." Ivy pursed her lips. "She's been a good friend already, and yet she barely knows me."

"She's a warm-hearted soul who has never met a stranger." Memories of his first days in Lincoln washed into his mind. "She was the same with me when I arrived." He pulled on the horse's reins. "Whoa." The wagon rolled to a stop in front of the two-story clapboard house, and Slade jumped to the ground, then trotted to Ivy's side. "I know you won't let me carry you, but at least lean on me."

Her cheeks pinked as she climbed down, then gripped his arm. "You'll find out soon enough, so I'll let you know I do tend toward stubbornness, but in this case, I'm happy to let you help me. I'm more exhausted than I'd like to admit."

He slipped one arm around her waist, and he laced his fingers with her left hand. "Stubbornness can be an admirable trait here in the West as long as it doesn't become bullheadedness."

She grinned. "Which is a fine line, I would imagine."

He chuckled as he led her toward the steps. "Yes, and I may struggle with that a bit."

She joined him in laughter, and his chest swelled. A sweet woman with a delightful sense of humor, yet a will of steel. As beautiful on the inside as she was physically. God had outdone Himself.

The door opened, and Dinah rushed onto the porch. "You're here! Slade, bring her into the parlor and put her on the sofa. Wrap her in the quilt, and I'll be in with refreshments. I wasn't sure what she liked to eat, so I've made several different dishes."

"Formidable is right," Ivy whispered as she leaned toward him.

Her hair tickled his cheek, and a floral scent wafted into his nose. His gut tightened. How could she affect him so soon after meeting? He couldn't form a coherent thought, so he simply smiled as they made their way up the stairs and onto the porch.

Dinah enveloped them both in a quick hug, then whirled and held open the door.

They entered the house, and his booted feet clomped on the gleaming wood floor. Ivy sagged against him.

He braced her more firmly. "Are you sure you shouldn't go to your room? You seem to be flagging."

She shook her head, her lips a thin line. "Once I'm on the sofa, and have some food in me, I should be fine. Really."

"All right, but I reserve the right to send you to bed."

"Hmmm, you *are* stubborn." She raised one eyebrow, and a smile tugged at one corner of her mouth. "We'll see."

He led her into the parlor, a room decorated in shades of blue. Sunlight streamed through the windows and puddled onto the floor. Wood was stacked in the fireplace, ready to be lit at a moment's notice despite it being August. Dinah was nothing if not prepared for every contingency. He settled Ivy on the couch and tucked the quilt around her, the fragrance of her hair again filling his senses. He cleared his throat. "Comfortable?" He was close enough to see the gold flecks in her blue eyes.

"Yes, and I'd offer to pour if I thought you'd let me." She gave him a saucy smile. "But I will allow you to wait on me this one time."

"You are a sassy one." He grinned, then pressed a kiss to her forehead before he could change his mind. His lips tingled from the warmth of her skin, and his pulse raced. His gaze dropped to her pink, kissable lips. He gulped. Space. He needed to put some space between them before he did anything foolish. "How do you take your tea?"

"With a bit of sweetener, if you don't mind."

"No milk?"

She wrinkled her nose. "No."

He quickly made Ivy's tea as Dinah hurried into the room followed by the cook. Both women carried trays laden with food. He crossed the room and gave Ivy the tea. Their hand brushed, and the tingling on his mouth was joined with more tingling that shot from his fingertips to his elbow. His eyes widened, and he met Ivy's gaze. Did she feel that, too?

Behind him, Dinah and the cook moved the platters of food from the trays to the sideboard against the wall. Savory and sweet smells mingled in a delectable combination, and Slade's mouth watered. "Would you like me to tell you the choices or bring you a selection?"

"I trust you."

His spine straightened. Simple words, but significant after such a short time together. "Yes, you can." Did she understand the deeper meaning of his statement? He pivoted and went to the table. "You've outdone yourself, ladies. Just what our girl needs to regain her strength."

"Nothing special, Mr. Pendleton." The woman beamed. "Good wholesome food."

"Exactly." He quickly put a bite or two from each dish onto Ivy's plate, then filled a plate for himself. "Will you be joining us, Dinah?"

"No, I don't believe there is a need for a chaperone." She nudged his shoulder. "Mrs. Tewksbury and I have some canning to do." Like Ivy, Dinah came from wealth, but she rolled up her sleeves and was involved in every aspect of running the house, often performing the tasks herself or in partnership with the staff. In the beginning, her employees had found her presence disconcerting but soon enjoyed the camaraderie. He sought to emulate Nathan and Dinah on his own ranch.

"I'll be here long enough to ensure she eats, then will call you when she's ready to retire."

Dinah patted his arm, then motioned for Mrs. Tewksbury to precede her out of the room. After they went, Slade carried the plates to the sofa and handed one to Ivy. It was tempting to join her on the sofa, but they both needed space. Her to recover. Him to analyze his reactions to her nearness. She'd only been in Lincoln for a week, but his senses were already tuned to her presence. Highly tuned. He cleared his throat. "Don't feel like you have to eat everything on your plate or be sociable."

She nodded as she nibbled on one of the tiny sandwiches. Color had returned to her face, and she looked less fatigued, but she needed rest after the drive to the ranch. They ate in silence for a couple of minutes, then she stilled.

He put aside his plate and jumped up. "Finished? Do you want me to call for Dinah to take you upstairs?"

"Yes, I'm finished, and no, I'd like to sit here for a while." She smiled. "You don't need to treat me like a porcelain doll. I'm fine. Tired, but fine."

Slade stacked her plate on his, then walked across the room and set them on the table. He returned and lowered himself in the chair he'd vacated. "I'm pleased you're recovering."

"I hear what you're not saying. This was not your fault, so stop blaming yourself. I've already forgiven you as you asked, even though there is nothing to forgive." Her eyes sparkled. "I do want to learn more about your ranch and life here in Lincoln. Both are foreign to what I experienced in Pennsylvania." Her lips twisted. "Our dangers are of the two-legged variety."

"We have those here, too, and I'll be sure to warn you accordingly." He laced his fingers to keep from reaching for her hand. "I am sorry for what happened to you, but am glad Mrs. Crenshaw sent you to Nebraska. To me."

"As am I." She smoothed her skirts. "You've been most kind. And patient. Dinah and Nathan, too. They're dear people. I couldn't ask for better friends. They've treated me as family."

"They did the same for me."

"Before the, um, accident, Dinah had started to teach me about running the household. It's quite involved. I hope I'm able to learn it all."

"You're a bright gal. "I'm sure you'll get the hang of it."

Embarrassment flashed across her face. "We've also been studying the Bible. My faith faltered after Mama died, and Papa…" She shrugged. "Well, you know."

"I do, but you're safe with us. With me." If only she'd agree to marry him sooner rather than the thirty days. He could only protect her best if they were wed. Then there was nothing her father or the snake who wanted to marry her could do. "You're safe," he repeated.

"I know. Dinah has assured me." She nibbled her lower lip. "But I'm struggling to forgive Papa. He was desperate, but he'd ignored me for the most part since Mama's passing. Years of neglect, then suddenly, he sees me as a way out of his problem. His sinful problem. Shame on him." Her voice hardened. "Dinah says I should forgive him, but I can never do so. Never." She looked mulish.

"I understand, and you must come to your own decision, but I have learned that holding on to bitterness only hurts me. Your papa isn't affected. He doesn't know how you feel, but your hate will change who you are."

Ivy huffed out a sigh. "I'll think about what you've said, but it won't be easy."

"No, it won't, but God will be with you, and so will I." Would she allow him to guide her, or would she see him as another man telling her what to do?

Chapter Eight

Sweat trickled down Slade's back as he gripped the roll of prickly barbed wire while Monty drove another spike into the ground on which to affix the fencing. It had been four years since Joseph Glidden had patented his simple wire barb into a double-strand wire, but Slade never took it for granted. He'd spent too much time chasing loose cattle and repairing the single strand version that broke against the animals' weight in the early days of his ranch.

He and Monty had gotten a late start, and the sun was nearly at its zenith, but the ride to Nathan's place to check on Ivy had been worth it. Although surprised to see him, she'd greeted him with a wide smile, her crystal-blue eyes sparkling with delight. She walked with only a slight limp as she favored her tender ankle, but she seemed to suffer no ill effects as she poured his coffee and plated muffins for the two of them to share.

She assured him that she was taking it easy, but Dinah was allowing her to do some of the easier chores per the doctor's instructions.

Was it too soon to be working? Doctors were smart, but they didn't know everything. What if she overdid and strained the wounds? What if she regressed?

As they talked and ate, time had gotten away from him, and before he knew it two hours had passed, the coffee and pastries long gone. If Dinah hadn't come in to ask for Ivy's help folding laundry, he might still be there. Dinah had teased him about overstaying his welcome, but he knew she was just giving him sass. She was one of the most kindhearted women in Lincoln. When he'd returned to the ranch, Monty had quipped about priorities and burning daylight. At nearly sixty, the man was old enough to be Slade's father and had treated him like a son since the moment he'd ridden onto the ranch. His plainspoken wisdom had solved more than a few issues, but now it seemed Slade's personal life was under inspection.

"Ow!" Monty yelped. "Hey, boss, pay attention."

Slade's face heated. "Sorry, Monty."

"You know what, let's take a break. We've been at this for a while."

"No, I'm good. We need to get it finished. It's bad enough that I put us behind."

"Just a few minutes." Monty dropped the hammer, then pulled off his Stetson and wiped the sweat from his face with his sleeve. He bent and picked up one of the canteens, then drank deeply before replacing the cap. "We've made decent progress, and these old bones could use a stretch."

"Ha, old, nothing." Slade grabbed another canteen and sipped the tepid water. "You put some of the younger bucks to shame."

Monty grinned. "That I do, but it's a matter of pride. Can't let them show me up. I'm not ready to be put out to pasture."

Slade removed his leather gloves, then clapped his foreman on the shoulder. "You've got a place here as long as you want it. Don't worry about that."

"I appreciate it." Monty fanned his face with his hat. "I don't mean no harm, boss, but you gotta focus on the job. I only got nicked, but another time of you not focusin' could cause a world of hurt."

"Yeah, about tha—"

"What's on your mind? Hopefully, nothin' more serious than that mail-order bride you've got stashed at Mr. Childs's place. She sure is a sweet thing."

"Yes, she is." Slade shrugged. "I worry about her. She's still recovering from the snake bite, yet she's helping Dinah with tasks. Is it too soon? Should she be in bed? To be honest, I'm afraid she's going to realize this isn't a fit, that she never should have come West."

"Sounds like you're startin' to care about the little lady. That's good. Most of these mail-order marriages don't start with any feelings, and that's a tough way to begin married life. At a minimum there should be mutual respect, but it's love that will carry you through the hard times.

You gotta treat her special, and when you find one you want to do that for, there's nothing like it."

Slade raised one eyebrow. "Sounds like the voice of experience, Monty. Were you married? *Are* you married?"

"I was. Best ten years of my life. We were never able to have children, so it was just the two of us, but then she was killed in a carriage accident." He swiped at his eyes. "She lingered for three days until succumbin' to her injuries, and I tried to negotiate with God not to take her, but I guess He wanted her more than me."

A long silence stretched between them. Overhead, a hawk screeched as it swooped in the breeze. Slade cleared his throat. "And you never remarried?"

"Nope." Monty shook his head as he stared off into the distance. "No one can ever take her place. Some people can remarry. Can find a love like we had a second time around, but that's not me. Sure, I get lonely, but not lonely enough to marry again." He blinked and leveled his gaze on Slade's face. "But it's still early for you and Miss Cregg. You gotta invest yourself into courtin' her. She seems like a fine woman. Don't let her get away."

"I'm not sure I remember how to court. I left all that behind in England."

"You don't have to do anything fancy. Take a walk. Sit on the porch. Read to her. Have dinner with her. You want to get to know each other. That's the key to a strong marriage. Knowing each other so good you can finish the other's sentence." Monty tilted his head and narrowed his eyes. "Have you prayed about the situation? About her? If you're gonna be head of the house, you need to pray for her and with her."

An easy laugh vibrated in Slade's chest. Monty was the only one he let be so candid with him. He deserved a candid answer. "Um, not as much as I should. I'm floundering here. I don't know what to ask."

"That's all right, son. He knows. He just wants to hear from you. Tell Him exactly what you just said to me, but you know that. You've been a believer longer than me."

"I'm going to start calling you Preach."

Monty snorted a laugh. "Not a label I'm keen on. Now, the men and I have heard you and the young lady have given this relationship thirty days, so there's less than three weeks remainin.' Courtin' her is what you should be focused on. The boys and I can handle the ranch."

"I daresay you're right." Slade donned his gloves. "Managing a couple thousand head of cattle is much easier than wooing one woman. I'll be counting on your prayers."

"Already on it, son. Already on it."

Ivy's Inheritance

Chapter Nine

Seated at the kitchen table, Ivy folded the mountain of laundry Dinah had brought inside from the line. Her friend still babied her despite Ivy's protestations that she could stand long enough to unclip the clothes and drop them into the basket. Or two. How could a family of three and one guest produce so many soiled garments? She had a new appreciation for the maids in Papa's house who'd kept fresh clothing in her chifferobes and armoires.

She stared out the window and sighed. Had the skies in Pennsylvania been as dazzling as this morning's cloudless blue expanse? With all the buildings, it certainly hadn't been as visible. The cornfields glowed under sun's rays. Were colors brighter in Nebraska, or was it her new lease on life that brightened the view?

It hardly seemed possible that only ten days had passed since she'd fled her home state. So much had changed in such a short period of time: more than just the callouses that were forming on her palms from washing clothes, scrubbing dishes, and harvesting a vegetable garden. She was different on the inside. Not as different as she wanted yet, but she was on her way.

Watching Dinah manage the household with a gracious firmness brought distant memories to the surface of the times her mother had provided guidance about a particular task or social custom, but then Mama was gone, and Ivy faded into the background. Especially after the women who hoped to capture Papa's heart and his fortune came calling. Nibbling her lower lip, Ivy shook her head. Enough ruminating about the past. She couldn't forgive him for selling her off like some prized cow, but what he'd done set her on a new path, perhaps even better than she would have had in Pennsylvania.

Tearing her eyes away from the beautiful landscape, she glanced at Nathan's shirt in her lap, then quickly folded the garment and piled it with the rest on the end of the table. What would it be like to fold Slade's clothing? Her face warmed at such an intimate thought.

Heavy footsteps sounded, and she turned to the doorway. Nathan should be in the fields, and none of the ranch hands ever came into the house.

As if conjured by her earlier musings, Slade appeared on the threshold, his tanned face wreathed in smiles. He held something behind his back. She started to rise, but he motioned for her to remain seated.

Her pulse raced, but she'd think about that later. "To what do I owe the pleasure?"

"Close your eyes."

"What?"

"I've brought you a surprise. Close your eyes."

Giggling, she squeezed her eyelids. "Shouldn't you be watching the cattle?"

He chuckled. "I've got a bunch of hands to do that. No peeking."

"I'm not."

The floor squeaked as he walked toward her, then his masculine scent of leather, sweat, and the unique aroma she'd come to associate with him enveloped her nose. A rod of some sort was placed in her hands.

"Okay, you can open your eyes."

She looked at the gleaming cane in her lap and gasped. "Oh, Slade, it's beautiful. Did you make this?"

He looked pleased as he rocked on his heels. "Yes, I learned to carve from one of the men in my platoon. Anyway, it will help you get around while you're still healing. You must be sick of being housebound."

Pressing the cane to her chest, she nodded. "I was just sitting here feeling sorry for myself. Doing chores while it's such a gorgeous day outside, but Dinah warned me about trying to navigate the grounds because they might be uneven."

"Do you have other chores to complete when you've finished the laundry?"

"No, I'd planned to read."

"How about if I help you fold, then we can head into town to the mercantile where you can pick up supplies for school? The school board has an account there, so you won't be out of pocket for the expenditures."

Her eyes filled with tears, and she blinked them away. "I'm sorry, you must think me quite foolish for crying over a trip to town."

"Not in the least." He rested one hand on her shoulder. "You've had a lot of change in the last two weeks, to say nothing of getting bit by a snake. And even though you wanted to leave Pennsylvania, you must be fighting a little bit of homesickness. It wasn't all bad, was it?"

"No, it wasn't." The warmth of his touch permeated her blouse, and she shivered as she gave him a wobbly smile. "You'd like my friend Alma. We had many happy times together. She's the one who helped me sneak things out of the house, then escape. I'm afraid we were quite illicit with our activities, claiming that she was collecting cast-off gowns for the poor."

"I'm sure God has forgiven you." He clomped to the other side of the table, lowered himself in the chair, then winked. "You're going to have to tell me what to do. Laundry isn't exactly my forte."

"We'll have to change that." She laid the cane on the floor beside the chair. "But first, um, thank you for all you've done for me thus far. You've saved my life, twice. Once from my father's machinations and once from a snake. You barely know me, yet you've done so much."

He patted her hand. "And I'd do it all again. You're safe here."

"But Mr. Heisel has money, lots of money. Enough to put out a hefty reward for my return."

"We have something much stronger. Someone. God is on our side. He'll ensure your safety."

"How can you be sure?" She twisted her fingers together. "Really sure?"

"Because you're one of His children, and He takes care of His own. That's not to say nothing bad ever happens to believers, but I'm going to step out in faith and say He does not want you tied to that man."

Ivy swallowed the lump that had formed in her throat. Could she trust God? Could she trust Slade? He was nothing like Papa had claimed. Many a time she'd heard him state that Englishmen had no honor. Ten days in, and Slade had proven himself nothing but trustworthy. Was anything she'd learned while growing up to be believed?

Slade selected a denim shirt from the basket as he watched uncertainty flit across Ivy's face. He'd said enough, so he would leave her alone with her thoughts. He hoped she'd come to believe his words. Her distraught expression tugged at his heart. She deserved a life of ease, not fear. Instead, she'd had to leave everything she knew to trek more than a thousand miles to become a rancher's wife. She had the tenacity. Of that he had no doubt. She's already shown herself to be of strong spirit. He'd seen more than a few families change their minds and return home in the East because they couldn't handle the harsh realities of life on the prairie. Difficult at best, unforgiving at its worst.

He buttoned the garment, then laid it face down on the table. A quick glance at Ivy showed her doing the same thing. So far, so good. She smoothed the fabric, so he made the same motions on his shirt, but the callouses on his palms caught the material, causing it to wrinkle. He pressed his lips together and used the back of one hand to flatten the shirt. Better, but not great. Another glance at Ivy revealed she'd already folded the shirt and was at work on another.

With a frown he bent over his task, alternately tugging and smoothing the shirt. Perspiration formed at his hairline. Finally satisfied, he folded the sleeves toward the center, then folded the garment in half. One shoulder was narrower than the other. He huffed out a sigh.

"You're doing fine, but you can just keep me company if you'd rather." Ivy's voice was gentle, encouraging. "I appreciate you making the effort. No man I've ever known has stooped to doing laundry."

Slade looked up, and his gaze strayed to the stack of shirts at her elbow. He grinned. "Apparently, I'm slowing you down, and it's not as easy as you make it appear."

"You should have seen my first attempts. Dinah was very patient." She giggled and lifted one shoulder in a delicate shrug. Her fingers flew as she plucked an item from the basket, folded it, then added the garment to the growing pile. "You have other skills." She folded another item. Now, how about if you tell me about the mercantile. Is it like department stores in Philadelphia?"

Chuckling, he crossed his arms. "Similar but not quite. From what I know about department stores, they have three or four sectioned areas devoted to a particular product such as hats. The mercantile has everything from fabric and clothes to canned goods, tools, and feed, but there are no defined departments per se."

Finished folding the clothes, Ivy sat back in the chair and brushed a stray hair off her forehead. Her face was flushed, but her eyes sparkled, so perhaps she was simply warm from working rather than not feeling well. She bent to retrieve the cane. "Does the shop carry guns and ammunition?"

"Yes, of course." He raised one eyebrow. "In the market for a gun?"

"I thought it might be a good idea if I learned how to shoot. You won't always be around. I need to be able to defend myself now that I'm out West." She pushed back her chair, leaned on the cane, and rose. "There's nothing like the present, don't you think?"

He gaped at her for a long moment, then scrambled to his feet. "Well, yes, I suppose." He peered at her. "Are you certain you've rested sufficiently? It will require some strength."

She raised her chin, and a dogged expression settled on her face. "Quite certain." She motioned to the laundry. "I'm grateful for all Dinah and Nathan have done for me, and I'll continue to help with household chores, but I'm sick to death of being inside. I must begin to learn what I must know to survive here. I can't count on someone to be in the vicinity to save me."

He held up his hands in surrender. "Understood. I not trying to mollycoddle you… Well, maybe I am. I simply don't want you to regress. A snake bite is a serious injury." Slade pursed his lips. "I'm overreaching, aren't I? My authority, I mean. I have no say over you. We're not betrothed or even committed. I'm sorry—"

"There's no need to apologize. You've been nothing but solicitous. I sense no ulterior motive, but of course, I've been fooled before." A frown darkened her cheeks for a moment, then cleared. "We both want this to succeed, so let's work toward that end. We'll take things one day at a time. And today is the day you teach me to shoot."

The tightness in his chest eased. Perhaps he hadn't totally bungled things, and there was a glimmer of hope that she'd remain in Lincoln to become his wife. "Right, then let's get to it. Dare I offer my arm as a support, Miss I-Can-Do-Things-For-Myself?"

Ivy snickered and sent him a saucy smile. "I would deign to accept your assistance."

"Excellent." Slade grinned and rushed around the table, then crooked his arm. Ivy slipped her left hand into the bend of his elbow, and the crisp scent of her soap mingled with the fragrance of lavender. He tamped down the desire to dip his head to inhale deeply. Instead, he straightened his spine and allowed her to lead him out the door that led to the back of the house. Standing close to her and remaining aloof while teaching her to shoot would prove to be exquisite agony. Ten short days, and she'd already taken up residence in his heart. How had that happened? Would she reciprocate his feelings? Time would tell, and he was not a patient man. Lord help them both.

Ivy's Inheritance

Chapter Ten

Squinting against the sun as she tried to focus on the tip of the Colt's barrel, Ivy tightened her fingers on the handle of the gun that Slade told her was called the grip. She'd lost track of how long she and Slade had been outside. It could be thirty minutes or two hours. Somewhere in between, if she was correctly reading how far the ball of fire had dipped since starting the lesson. Perspiration trickled between her shoulder blades and slicked her palms.

She'd gotten over her fear of the weapon's explosion. Well, mostly. She only slightly flinched when the gun fired. Her arms trembled from the weight, but pride kept her from telling Slade she was getting tired. If she was to survive on the prairie, she needed to be strong, and that came from lots of practice.

"Another round of shots, then we'll quit." Behind her, Slade leaned close and spoke in her ear. "You've done well."

His breath brushed her cheek, and she shivered. Once again, she was stunned at how his proximity affected her after less than two weeks together. But affect her he did.

"Ready?" Slade touched her back, sending more shivers through her body.

"Yes." She took a deep breath. His instructions were drilled into her head. Brace her right hand with her left, hold her finger along the side of the weapon until ready to shoot, point the barrel at her target lining up the sight, cock the hammer, then squeeze the trigger. He'd been adamant about that last part. Squeezing, not jerking or tugging. Would firing the weapon ever become second nature?

Ivy performed the steps and managed to hit four of the six cans he'd lined up on the log. She grinned as he cheered her success. Pointing the gun toward the ground, she handed Slade the weapon, and he slid it into his holster.

"That's my girl." Slade drew her into a quick hug, then seemed to realize what he'd done and released her as if burned. Face flushed, he said, "Congratulations."

Lowering herself into a curtsy, she couldn't stop smiling. "Thank you, kind sir. I'm nowhere as proficient as I want, but I'll get there. If you had told me a month ago, I'd be standing in the middle of a field shooting a gun, I would have laughed in your face."

"Life can change on a dime." He pushed his Stetson back on his head. "I'm glad to be able to help you, Ivy. When we go to the mercantile, we'll purchase your weapon, and after you're comfortable with it, we'll pull out my Winchester and teach you how to shoot a rifle."

"A rifle?" Her voice squeaked. "I don't—"

"We won't start until you're ready, but you should know how to fire one." He patted her shoulder. "It's not as terrifying as you think. Like with the pistol, it's a matter of knowing how to handle it safely and effectively. A gun is merely a tool. Granted, a dangerous tool, but you have control, and I won't let you get injured."

Licking her lips, she nodded. He hadn't led her astray yet. What would Alma say if she could see Ivy now?

"Let Dinah know we're borrowing the wagon while I hitch up Midnight. Take time to change your dress if you'd like." He handed her the cane. "I think you look lovely, but I've learned from Dinah that you ladies have certain expectations about what to wear and when to wear it."

"I definitely want to freshen up. I shouldn't be more than a few minutes."

"Take your time."

She took the cane from his hands, and their fingers brushed, and the tingles she'd come to expect shot to her elbow. Did he feel them? If they married, would it always be like this? "Th-thanks. I'll meet you out front in fifteen minutes."

Hurrying into the house, cane clacking on the floor, she brushed a stray lock of hair away from her face. Slade said she looked lovely, yet disheveled was more likely. She climbed the stairs and entered the bedroom. A quick glance in the mirror confirmed her suspicions about her appearance, and she shook her head. She was as far from lovely as possible. A smudge of dirt marred her left cheek, and her hair frizzled around her face. Her collar was dark with perspiration. Ugh. The man must have cataracts.

Ivy tossed the cane onto the bed, then poured water from the pitcher into the ewer and quickly stripped to her underclothes. In moments, she'd cleaned and dried her body before donning her favorite blue skirt and blouse. The garments were old but had held up well and were comfortable. She unpinned her hair, brushed out the dark strands, then plaited a single braid and wound it around her head. She did not miss the time and effort to create elaborate hairstyles necessary in Drexel Hill society. The clock downstairs chimed the hour. She whirled, grabbed the cane, and rushed out the door and down the hall as fast as her tender ankle would let her, then stopped at the top of the stairs. She might be on the prairie, but a lady did not run through the house like a banshee. And Slade and Dinah would not be happy if they knew she wasn't favoring her leg. Smoothing her skirts, she descended the stairs, then turned toward the kitchen. Entering the room, she only found the cook. "Have you seen Mrs. Childs?"

"Oh, honey, we don't stand on that kind of ceremony here. It's Dinah, and she headed out to the fields. Something about needing to see Nathan."

"Would you let her know that Mr. Pendle…I mean, Slade and I are going to town, and we've borrowed the wagon. In fact, we're headed to the mercantile. Do you need anything?"

"Kind of you to ask, but nothing pressing, so just go and enjoy yourself." Mrs. Tewksbury peered at her. "You sure you feel up to making the trip?"

"I think so. And Slade will ensure I don't overdo."

The cook smiled. "That he will. Such a delightful young man. Make him take you to dinner. Now, shoo. I'll give the missus your message."

"Thank you!" Skirts rustling, Ivy gave up being sedate and hurried through the corridor. She yanked open the front door. Slade stood on the porch, his hand stretched toward the knob. They both yelped, then chuckled. She pressed a hand against her chest. "I'm late. I said fifteen minutes. I promise—"

Slade patted her shoulder. "Relax. We're not on a schedule."

"But you were coming into the house."

"Because I'd rather wait inside than keep Midnight company." He grinned, then scooped her into his arms. "Who needs a cane when you've got me?"

She squealed, and the laughter in his chest rumbled in her ear. The man never ceased to surprise her. Her initial estimation of a stuffy Englishman had been totally wrong. Her heart beat wildly, and she licked her dry lips. Did she need the next two weeks to make her decision? Why was she hesitating?

He marched down the steps, then set her on her feet near the wagon. Gripping her hand, he helped her climb into the vehicle. He walked to the horse and spoke a few quiet words into his ear, then stroked Midnight's nose. With a whinny, the horse raised and lowered his head as if agreeing with whatever Slade had said.

As he settled beside her on the bench, she glanced at him. "You've quite a way with animals."

His cheeks flushed, and he shrugged. "God gave us stewardship over them. Treat them well, and they'll serve you unswervingly. And truth be told, sometimes I prefer them to my fellow man."

Ivy snickered.

Slade flicked the reins, and the wagon rolled forward. As they made their way through toward town, he entertained her with more stories of his early days of ranching and the history of Lincoln. Time passed quickly, and before she knew it, they were approaching town. Shouts, laughter, and the rattle of wagons floated on the air toward her. The streets and sidewalks teemed with activity. Her heart swelled. Not Drexel Hill, but large enough. She bounced on the seat like a child on the way to the circus.

"Excited to be here?" Slade winked at her. "I may never get you back to Dinah's."

"I do love the chaos associated with cities and large towns, but it's always nice to return to the quiet of one's home afterwards." Her eyes scanned the signage above each shop. "Where is the mercantile?"

He pointed to a standalone building with a bright green sign that swung from wrought-iron hangers. The store outgrew their space twice, so the owner constructed that last year."

Her eyes widened. "Impressive. They would give Wanamaker's a run for their money."

"A store where you live?"

"Philadelphia. They have dozens of departments. Men and women come from miles around to shop there."

Slade parked the wagon in front of the store, then jumped to the ground and lashed the reins around the hitching post before helping Ivy down from the vehicle. His nearness sent her pulse racing, and she pursed her lips. Twenty-five years old yet responding like a schoolgirl. She raised her chin and unsuccessfully tried to ignore the shiver running down her spine. Hopefully, he wouldn't notice.

A frown appeared on his forehead. "Everything all right?"

Drat. So much for not noticing her discomfort. "Fine. Just excited, like you said."

He studied her face, then chuckled and led her inside.

A conglomeration of odors assailed her, and she took a deep breath. The vinegary smell of pickles mingled with the rich, sweet smell of leather. An earthy aroma of potatoes and mustiness pervaded the room. Other smells she couldn't identify. Definitely not Wanamaker's with their pneumatic ventilation system, but just as much of a treasure trove. Her gaze bounced from one display to the next. Where to start?

"Slade! *Gut* to see you. *Ja,* and I was just considering sending someone out to the ranch." Luther Vestal, the manager of the mercantile threaded his way through the racks, a newspaper gripped in one hand. When he reached them, he dipped his head. "Nice to see you, Miss Cregg." His gray eyes were clouded. "I'm afraid I've got some bad news." He snapped open the newspaper, and Ivy gasped. A reproduction of the photograph her father had taken last year stared at her from the front page. In large black type, the headline screamed "REWARD FOR THE RETURN OF IVY CREGG."

Pinpricks of light appeared in Ivy's vision, and she swayed. She couldn't faint. Not now. Not before she read the article in its entirety. She took a deep breath, and her vision cleared. She spoke through clenched teeth: "What does it say?"

Slade looked thunderous. "Nonsense. Nothing but nonsense."

"What? You must tell me."

"The article alludes to mental health issues, and that you are to be considered dangerous to yourself and others. The reward is ten thousand dollars. Anyone who spots you is to send a telegram to Gareth Heisel and not try to take you back to Pennsylvania."

Ivy's eyes filled with tears, and her knees nearly buckled. How could this happen? Didn't Slade promise that God would keep her safe?

Slade wrapped an arm around her waist keeping her upright. He gestured at a nearby chair, then helped her to it and lowered her on the seat.

She shuddered and wrapped her arms around her middle as she raised brimming eyes toward Slade. "They found me. I didn't think they'd find me."

"No. If I was a betting man, I'd say this piece is running in towns and cities across the nation. He's fishing."

"So much money. Someone in Lincoln is going to turn me in." She clutched at her skirts. "I must go. I'm putting you and everyone here in danger. I must return. He won't rest until he gets what he wants. Me, in marriage."

"Absolutely not." Slade pounded on the counter. "He's the one who is dangerous. I've seen his ilk before. You would not be safe wed to that man." He dropped to one knee in front of her. "I know you asked for thirty days, but I don't believe we have that luxury. Please marry me. That will solve the problem. If we're married, he'll have no recourse."

Ivy gulped. "You don't know that. He is powerful, and he has money. Can he get a judge to annul the marriage? Make me marry him?"

"We'll speak to an attorney." He cradled her hands in his, the warmth of his skin enveloping her. "You are not alone. We are not alone." He glanced at Luther. "Thank you for bringing this to our attention. You could have turned her in."

"Hardly." The man shook his head. "I, too, have seen scoundrels like this man. He doesn't deserve sweet Miss Cregg. She's ours now."

Despite the seriousness of the situation, Ivy smiled. Who knew if the man spoke for everyone, but her heart warmed at his sentiments. Was God using the man to tell her everything would work out? She wanted to believe that. *Please, God, let it be true.*

Chapter Eleven

Clutching her reticule, Ivy stared at the bushy eyebrows, no, *eyebrow*, of the attorney. She stifled a grin. One long eyebrow met at the bridge of the man's nose and looked like a caterpillar had taken up residence on his forehead. Did he not know how ridiculous he appeared? Perhaps not. He'd been droning on for fifteen minutes without actually saying anything, clearing his throat numerous times and assuring them he'd investigate their case. How hard was it to know marriage law. Or was it contract law?

A sigh slipped out, and Slade shot a glance in her direction. She sent him an encouraging smile, then turned her gaze back to the attorney. She pinned a smile on her face and tightened her grip on her small handbag. "Attorney Jurak, I'm sure you're a busy man, and we're loathe to take up more of your time, so if you could just confirm whether the agreement between my father and this man is valid. Am I required to marry him? I would like to believe that as a woman in her majority who had nothing whatsoever to do with the arrangement, I have rights. What say you?"

"You are over eighteen?" The attorney's eyebrow cleared. "And you didn't sign anything?"

"I am well over eighteen. Twenty-five, to be exact, and no, I didn't sign any documents, but frankly, I wouldn't put it past this scoundrel to forge my signature."

"That would be a problem. Yes, indeed, a large problem, especially if it is a professional forgery."

Ivy leaned forward. "You're telling me if he breaks the law, I could find myself married without my consent?"

"Well…" Mr. Jurak cleared his throat again and shuffled the stack of paper on his desk. "If he is nefarious and as rich as you say, it is possible. Money moves mountains, you know."

Climbing to her feet, Ivy dipped her head. "I do know. Slade, I believe I've heard enough." Her heart raced. What good was the law if someone could circumvent it?

Slade jumped up, and the chair legs scraped against the wooden floor. He cringed, then schooled his features and held out his arm. Gracious as always, he'd allowed her to guide the conversation. Not like other men who would take charge as if the situation were their issue. The attorney had initially directed his conversation and his gaze at Slade, but when he remained mute and motioned to Ivy, Mr. Jurak had finally met her eyes. She'd seen the doubt. He didn't think she was smart enough to understand. He wasn't the first man to underestimate her, nor would he be the last.

She slid her hand in the bend of Slade's elbow and murmured good day to the attorney. They strode from the office, then past the fresh-faced young law clerk and out the door. The heat hit her like an oven, and she wrinkled her nose. Fanning herself, she hesitated. What to do? Forego the mercantile and head back to Dinah's like a frightened rabbit or remain and do what she came to do?

Slade bent and whispered in her ear his breath tickling her cheek, "We've much to discuss, but a trip to the mercantile first. If we change our plans and cower, the rogue will have won, and we can't let that happen."

She straightened her spine. "Quite right." If it were only that simple.

He tugged her forward, and they threaded their way through the morning crowd. The heat was oppressive, and perspiration formed on Ivy's upper lip and pooled under her arms. Less humid than Pennsylvania's sticky summers, but hot, nonetheless. Fortunately, Dinah had assured her immediately that corsets weren't necessary out West, so Ivy had shed the binding bone-filled contraption without a backward glance. They entered the shop, and Ivy inhaled deeply as she waited for her eyes to adjust to the dim interior.

"Remember, the school board has said you may purchase whatever you need, so don't skimp."

"I should have taken inventory at the schoolhouse before coming here." She frowned. "But events prevented that. Should we head over there?"

"No. Even if you purchase items already in stock, you'll use them eventually. The parents are thrilled to have a new schoolteacher, so I expect enrollment to go up."

She blew out a loud breath. "But they don't know if I'm any good."

"A highly educated lady from Philadelphia society? You'll do just fine." Eyes dancing, he grinned and motioned toward a shelf that held a stack of slates and baskets of pencils. "Shiny new slates and crisp new pencils. What's not to love about that?"

His excitement was infectious, but she hesitated. What if she purchased items, then had to leave, whether of her own volition to escape or because the agreement proved to be valid. Nausea swept over her. May it never be! Could she return the items for a refund? She'd brought money of her own. She could pay the board for their losses. Either way, she was trapped.

"I see your mind working. You're considering fleeing. Leaving town and trying to hide out somewhere." Slade grabbed her hand and pulled her close. "You can't spend the rest of your life looking over your shoulder. Not allowing yourself happiness because you're afraid it will be yanked out from under you."

Tears welled in her eyes. Such a kind man, but he didn't deserve to be caught up in her woes.

"And don't say I shouldn't get involved."

She gaped at him. Was she that easy to read?

"Look, I know you're used to handling things on your own, but you have friends here. And me. I won't let anything happen to you. In fact, I think we should send a message to that man asking how much he'll take to dissolve the agreement."

Her jaw dropped farther. "You would purchase me?"

"No, nothing like that. We are ensuring your freedom."

Ivy shook her head. "He's greedy. He'll want too much money. I don't understand why you're willing to do this. You barely know me."

"Ivy, freedom is a precious thing. It's worth every nickel." He stroked her cheek. "And I know enough."

She fingered one of the slates. "I don't—"

"Another thing. Until this is resolved, you cannot be alone. Me or one of my men must be with you at all times."

"What? No."

"It's either that, or we tell the board school will be held at my ranch. We can see people approaching. I'll have one of the hands use the wagon to collect the children. The board doesn't need to know the real reason. We can say that the trip to town is still too much for you."

"Well—"

"Or we could solve this once and for all and marry immediately."

Her fingers flew to her mouth. "Marry? Now?"

His eyes clouded, and he shrugged. "It was just an idea, but the decision is entirely up to you."

Her throat thickened. She'd hurt Slade with her response, and all he'd ever done since her arrival was take care of her. Why couldn't Papa have been a real father? Instead, his gambling and poor choices had painted her into a corner. Which answer was the right one?

Chapter Twelve

Early morning sunlight seeped through the clouds overhead as the wagon rolled to a stop in front of the schoolhouse. A warm breeze brushed Ivy's cheeks and lifted her bangs. She slanted her gaze at Slade who was busy setting the brake. His shoulder muscles rippled under his shirt with the motion. She gulped and looked away. Since when did she notice a man's physique? Truth be told, since she'd arrived in Lincoln, and Slade had greeted her at the station.

But he was more than a handsome man. His kindness and compassion with everyone he came into contact with from his animals to his ranch hands to store clerks. And her. He'd been gracious and warm from the moment they'd met. Was she only drawn to him because her soul was thirsty for gentleness and affection? Or were her feelings more deeply rooted?

Ivy waited while Slade jumped to the ground, then came around to her side. He smiled up at her as he extended his hand to help her down. She licked her lips, then grasped his fingers as she lifted her skirt, then climbed from the vehicle. Her pulse thrummed. From his nearness? From her excitement at finally beginning school?

He reached into the wagon and grabbed the pail she'd filled with food for the two of them. She'd lost the argument about having someone with her at all times, and he insisted on being the one to accompany her today. Surely, he had more important duties than babysitting her. Although, it would be worse if she took one of his paid hands from doing chores around the ranch.

"Ready?" He motioned toward the schoolhouse. "You couldn't have asked for a prettier day."

She nodded. "A mixed blessing, to be sure. Would you want to be stuck inside at school on such a nice day?"

"If my teacher was as lovely as you?" He winked. "Absolutely."

Shaking her head, she swatted his arm. "You've certainly become a silver-tongued devil."

His face flushed, and he shrugged. "I meant every word. Has no one ever told you that you are a beautiful, Ivy? A shame, if not."

It was her turn to blush, and she shook her head. "Mama, when I was little, but that's what mothers do. Papa was short on compliments. He probably didn't want me to become vain. Too many of the girls in society preened as if royalty. He said it was unbecoming."

"He's right, but that doesn't mean he shouldn't make you feel special. Anyway, enough about your father. Today is about you and the children." He withdrew the keys from his pocket and jingled them at her. "I'm sure you'd like to do the honors."

"Oh, yes." She snatched the ring and hurried toward the front door as she called over her shoulder. "I may not like that you're here because you think I need protecting, but I'm pleased to be sharing the moment."

"And I'm pleased to be the one sharing."

She opened the door and stepped inside. Close on her heels, Slade followed her into the room. She turned to say something and watched as his gaze ricocheted around the space. She frowned. "As you can see it is wide open with no closets or hiding places. I'm safe and sound."

"Yes, but one can never be too careful."

The aroma of chalk mingled with the sharp odor of vinegar. The church ladies had cleaned the building from top to bottom. Windows sparkled, and the large desk in front gleamed. Shelves were filled with books, and a pile of slates awaited the incoming students. She flung open her arms and twirled, her skirt billowing. "I thought this day would never come!"

He chuckled. "Were you this excited as a student?"

"I loved school. My whole world opened, especially through reading. So many wonderful stories to take me places I might never visit. I want to provide that for the children."

"And you will." Slade clapped his hands, the sound echoing in the vacant room. "You won't need it today, but the stove has been filled with kindling and paper, and a small supply of wood is in the shed out back. A group of men from church has committed to keeping the shed full, and your boys can retrieve the logs as necessary."

She cocked her head and tapped one finger on her cheek. Eyes twinkling, she said, "So, now you're telling me how to run my classroom?"

He laughed and held up his hands in surrender. "Far be it for me to do so."

"You better not." Giggling, she wagged her finger at him in mock sternness, then sobered. "Must you really stay? I appreciate all you've done for me. Are doing. But surely you have more important things to do either in town or on the ranch than to guard the new schoolmarm. Not every day."

"First, nothing is more important than you and your safety. Second, my men are quite capable of doing their jobs without me. For days and weeks at a time. One of the reasons I have a foreman and hire good staff." Slade rubbed the back of his neck. "And third, you've had a difficult beginning with us, and I want you to know this is a wonderful place to live. It can be the new start you're looking for. I got a new start, and so can you."

"Why would you need a new start?" She frowned. "I know you came from England. Were things so bad there?"

Shaking his head, he shoved his hands into the pockets of his denim pants. "Not there. Here. I came to America to fight in your civil war. It seemed a just cause, and it was, but I saw things. Terrible things." His voice broke, and he cleared his throat as he raised pain-filled eyes to her. "So much death and destruction. And evil. I saw men use the excuse of war to perform despicable acts. After it was over, I followed some of my unit mates out West. Ranches were hiring. The idea of working outdoors with horses and cattle who have no agenda, no mean spirits, touched a part of me that I thought died in the war. Best decision I ever made. I learned how to run a ranch, raise crops, and lead men. I scrimped and saved until I could purchase my own place." He smiled and shrugged. "So, I do know a bit about fresh starts."

Ivy's heart tugged. He'd experienced so many awful things, yet he was sad rather than bitter. "I was twelve when the war ended. Papa protected me from its ugliness by sending me to live with his sister, my aunt, in the far reaches of Maine. She and Papa had little in the way of a relationship, before or since, but she agreed to take me in. The only battle in Maine was the Battle of Portland Harbor, and we were hours from there. She and her husband lived off the land, so we wanted for nothing. After Lee's surrender, I was sent home. I wrote letters to her, but never received a response." She twisted her lips. "Perhaps she felt she'd done her duty and required no more interaction."

"We could visit if you wish." His voice was soft, caring.

She met his gaze. "That's kind of you, but that chapter of my life is over. As you say, a fresh start." She motioned to the desk. "For me and the children of Lincoln." Would she succeed?

Chapter Thirteen

"Thanks, Dinah." Slade snatched a warm oatmeal cookie from one of the pans on the kitchen counter, then grinned at Ivy who swatted his arm. "I'll see you ladies at dinner."

"Shame on you, Slade." Dinah snickered. "You'll ruin your appetite."

"Hardly. The man seems to have two hollow legs." Ivy shook her head. "You should have seen how much he put away at lunch. I can't believe he's hungry after that."

"Hey, I'm standing here, you know." He shot them both a look of mock offense. "I worked hard today helping her wrangle the students." Slade popped the cookie into his mouth, and flavor exploded on his tongue. He moaned and filched another treat as he swallowed.

Ivy batted her eyelashes, and her lips curled in a saucy smile. "You make a wonderful teaching assistant." She turned to Dinah. "Of course, the job wasn't all that tough. The girls had a crush on him, and the boys hero-worshipped him."

Slade's face warmed, and he shrugged. "Can I help it if I'm so impressive?"

"No, you can't." Ivy gave him a slight push. "Now, shoo so we can finish baking." She glanced at the watch pinned to her bodice. "Dinner's in an hour, and I'm sure Nathan could use some help until then."

"All right, I'm going, but I'll be back." Chuckling, he snatched a third cookie and twisted out of her reach, although he wouldn't mind another swat. With a wave he hurried from the kitchen, then down the corridor and out the front door.

Despite being late afternoon, the sun still hung high in the sky, casting shadows across the front of the house. He loved the long days, and he'd gotten used to the scorching heat of Kansas summers, so different from his native England. The vast plains were also different and beautiful in their own way, but he did miss the verdant forests of Britain. A small price to pay for the contentment he'd found in America. Would Ivy learn to love the state? He'd been through Pennsylvania during the brutal battles at Gettysburg and seen the grassy berms and wooded hills she'd grown up with.

Squinting against the glare, he surveyed the property as he thought about the day. Watching Ivy with the youngsters had been a joy. She obviously loved teaching, and she was good at it, explaining concepts in easy-to-understand ways and keeping the children's attention with a combination of encouragement and firmness. They'd sat rapt while she read from books she'd later told him were called McGuffey Readers. She'd explained the students would get their chance to read, but for the first day she wanted them to simply enjoy the story.

When the students got restless, she'd taken them outside for games, and afterwards, everyone sat in a circle eating their lunches. Each interaction she had with them provided a life lesson in a gentle but unassuming way. They hung on her every word. The experience was nothing like his own schooling so many years ago, with a series of teachers whose sole purpose seemed to be terrorizing their students. No warmth. Dry lectures given in monotone and paddling the boys for minor infractions. What would school have been like under the sweet tutelage of someone like Ivy?

Slade shook his head. Enough ruminating. Time to find Nathan and discuss the next steps to keep Ivy safe. He strode past the corral where two of the hands were attempting to break a majestic black stallion who seemed to be having none of it. The beast was gorgeous, his raven-colored hide nearly blue in the sunlight. Unless Slade missed his guess, the animal stood over eighteen hands high.

Dinah had indicated that Nathan was in the lower pasture branding the new calves. With any luck, he was almost done and would have time to talk. This was one conversation that shouldn't happen over dinner with the women. They'd both made it clear they thought he was overreacting about the newspaper article, and Ivy was safe in Lincoln. Slade knew better than that. Not with the amount of money being offered as a reward. Every man had his price, and ten thousand dollars was well above that price for most people.

Whistles and the bawling of cows floated toward him as he approached the pasture where several men wrestled calves to the ground and pressed the branding iron against the animal's hind quarter. Nathan caught sight of him and waved, then held up one finger. Excellent. They'd have time to talk.

Slade shoved his hands into his pockets, then propped one booted foot on the wooden enclosure. Nathan's staff had obviously worked together for a while, their motions practiced and almost choreographed. The wind shifted, sending the acrid aroma of burnt flesh and manure toward him. Also, nothing like the city of London he'd left behind.

Moments later, Nathan removed his leather gloves as he spoke to one of the men and jerked his head toward Slade. The man nodded, and Nathan strolled to the fence, then climbed over and landed on the ground sending a cloud of dust into the air. "How'd school go today?"

"No sign of danger, but it's only a matter of time." Slade pushed his Stetson back. "That's why I want to talk to you. Ivy's right that she can't be guarded every moment of every day. I've told her I've got staff to do the work, but honestly, you know what it takes to run a spread, and at the very least, I need to keep up with the books." He grimaced. "And I'm getting a little long in the tooth to be running on five hours of sleep for the foreseeable future."

Nathan narrowed his eyes. "What's your plan? Did you offer to marry her now?"

Sighing, Slade twisted his lips. "Yes, several times. She's having none of it."

"You want me to see if Dinah can persuade her?"

"No, but thank you," Slade said. "I also offered to contact the scoundrel and ask him how much he'd take to back off. To forget the agreement."

"And?"

"She was horrified. Felt like I'd be buying her, and that didn't sit well."

"I guess not." Nathan rocked on his heels. "So, what will you do?"

"Do you still keep in touch with your Pinkerton chaps? I'd like to hire a detective to go to Pennsylvania and size up the situation, seeing how far flung the articles have reached. Perhaps finagle his way into the lout's good graces to see what he can surmise about him. And Ivy's father." Slade slammed is palm against the fence and scowled. "What man sells his own daughter?"

"Unfortunately, that's been happening since time began."

"Doesn't make it right."

"No."

Slade took off his hat and slapped it against his thigh, then squinted at Nathan. "I have no doubt the man is dangerous. It's time to leave this to a professional. Do you have someone you can recommend? I've got money. I can pay."

"I've got just the man. It will take me a couple of days to contact him, and as long as he's not on another case, I know he'll help us out. Meanwhile, let's talk to my staff. I've only told them the bare minimum."

"Agreed. Same here. I'll address the situation at dinner tonight with my hands."

Nathan put two fingers to his lips and blew a piercing whistle. The men and beasts looked up, and Nathan motioned the hands close. They trotted to the fence, curiosity etched on their faces.

"Slade here has something to say, so listen up. Afterwards, I'll make my way around the ranch and inform the rest of the staff."

Slade cleared his throat. Could these men be trusted? Time would tell. "I don't know if you've seen the newspaper, but there's an article offering a reward for turning Ivy in to the authorities. Says she's dangerous and mad as a hatter. The reward is substantial. Ten thousand dollars." He leveled his gaze at the men, all of whom looked shocked. "People do stupid things for a lot less money. I'm asking you to be vigilant. Keep an eye out for strangers asking questions, coming onto the ranch for no reason, that sort of thing. I'm forced to trust you in this. You might be tempted to turn her in yourself, but don't. You keep my bride-to-be safe, and there'll be more than five thousand in it for you. Understood?"

"Yes, sir. You can count on us." One of the older hands tugged at his shirt collar. "Miss Ivy don't deserve that. She's been nothin' but kind to us."

"Thank you." Slade reached out and shook each of the men's hands over the fence. "Means a lot."

Nathan motioned to the calves that were milling around the corral. "Back at it, gents. Dinner in about thirty minutes." He looked at Slade. "I know my guys. They won't let you down."

Slade put on his hat and tugged it low on his forehead. "It's not them I'm worried about. I've no doubt this blackguard is wily. Will he pull one over on them?"

"Not if I can help it, friend. Not if I can help it."

Ivy's Inheritance

Chapter Fourteen

The kitchen door opened, and Slade clomped into the room with Nathan close on his heels. Startled, Ivy looked up from putting the final touches on a salad. Would she ever get used to the casual ways of the West? In Drexel Hill, servants came in through the back, not owners or their guests. The men removed their hats and hung them on hooks near the pantry, then Slade pumped water into the sink. The room suddenly felt half the size.

Slade smiled at her as he rolled up his sleeves, jostling Nathan with his shoulder. Like a pair of puppies, they pushed and shoved as they washed.

"Hey, keep your play outside, *boys.*" Dinah shook her finger at them in mock anger. "Can't have you knocking something over."

Pulse tripping, Ivy stared at Slade. The fabric of his shirt stretched across his broad back, the muscles bunching as he moved. On her left, Dinah snickered and jabbed her with an elbow. Ivy's face burned as she glared at her new friend, which only made Dinah laugh more.

The men stopped their roughhousing and glanced at them. Dinah waved in a dismissive gesture. "Just something between us girls. If one of you will pour the water, the other can start taking food to the table." She winked at Ivy, then turned and gave a final stir to the mashed potatoes.

Ivy pursed her lips and studied the salad. She was new to teasing. Joking had never happened in her father's household, even among the servants. Dinah, Nathan, and Slade ribbed each other regularly and sometimes mercilessly. The first time it happened, she'd been horrified, and all three had laughed uproariously. More so when they saw her discomfort. Then they'd apologized, but the provoking continued. She had yet to get into the swing of things. Would she ever?

She picked up the salad, then headed into the dining room where she set the bowl on the table. Nathan and Slade were huddled in the corner whispering between themselves. Nathan caught sight of her and clamped his mouth shut. He nudged Slade, this time in seriousness.

Her eyebrows shot up. What were they discussing they couldn't talk about in front of her? She wasn't aware of any aspect of ranch business that was secretive. She'd begun to trust Slade in the last few days. Was that trust misplaced?

"Best get back into the kitchen and retrieve the rest of the food. Nathan strode toward her, then slipped past. "Come on, Slade. There's plenty of work for all of us."

"Of course." Slade shrugged and hurried into the kitchen.

Ivy pivoted and followed the men. Something was definitely going on, but it would take some ferreting out if they were anything like her tight-lipped father, who only shared things when necessary. Were all men like that, or was it just her luck to get stuck?

Dinah handed her the gravy boat, then motioned to the large platter on which a large roast was surrounded by fragrant root vegetables. "If one of you gents will carry the main course…"

"I've got it, sweetheart." Nathan raised one hand, as if a pupil in Ivy's classroom, then marched to the stove and hefted the plate into his arms. "You've outdone yourself, as usual. Smells divine."

She pinked and shooed him and Slade out of the room, then picked up a large bowl of string beans. She rolled her eyes at Ivy. "They're in a mood tonight. I wonder what's gotten into them."

"I was just thinking the same thing. I caught the two of them in the dining room huddled in the corner whispering like two thieves."

"Don't worry. We'll find out. Nathan's not one for secrecy. I don't always like what he has to say, but he tells me everything. We're true partners. It will be like that for you with Slade."

"We'll see." Ivy shrugged, pinned on a smile, and walked into the dining room. She'd believe Dinah's words when Slade proved himself.

She'd thought Papa was honest and aboveboard until their world came crashing down because of his gambling and subterfuge. Slade would need to do more than be polite.

She set down the gravy with a thump, then shrugged at Slade's questioning glance. She'd never been one to hide her feelings, and she was annoyed at the men. Was she upset over nothing? Were there ever *good* secrets? Perhaps they were planning something nice for Dinah. Was her birthday coming up? After only two weeks, Ivy knew little about her friend.

Slade pulled out a chair for Ivy, and she stopped ruminating long enough to sit down. His manly scent of leather and sunshine tickled her nose. These men of the West who worked the land were nothing in appearance like the drawing-room gentlemen of the East, but did they crave the same things: money, property, and power? Both Nathan and Slade had massive ranches with thousands of cattle and acres of produce, to say nothing of their large, beautiful homes. They had the wealth and property. Did they have power? Power enough for people to be afraid to be honest about them? To a person, everyone she'd met claimed Slade was a good man who any woman would be lucky to marry.

"Would you say the blessing, Nathan?" Dinah said, breaking Ivy's reverie.

He nodded, and Ivy forced her attention to the words as he gave a quick prayer of thanksgiving before they began to eat. Ivy nearly moaned as she chewed the succulent bit of beef. Flavor exploded on her tongue, and the meat seemed to melt in her mouth. Cooking was another area in which she was deficient. Granted, Slade could afford a cook, but surely, he expected his wife to be able to feed him.

Silverware clinked on china, and conversation seasoned the meal as they discussed the ranch, events in town, and news about friends from church. Tension slipped from Ivy's shoulders as dinner progressed. Meals at home had been alternately lonely or contentious depending on Papa's attendance and mood. How long would it take her to heal?

Slade cleared his throat as he pushed away his empty plate, then wiped his mouth on the linen napkin. "Delicious as always, Dinah."

"Thank you, Slade. Did you get enough?"

"For now. I left room for that custard pie I saw on the counter."

"And you assumed it was for us tonight?"

His face flushed. "Well—"

Dinah snickered and rose. "I'm kidding. Of course, it's tonight's dessert. What's a meal without a treat at the end?"

He blew out a loud breath and rolled his eyes. "You do keep a man on his toes."

"Then my work here is done." She grinned and picked up the soiled dishes as Nathan climbed to his feet to help her. "You two enjoy your coffee. We'll take care of this."

Ivy pushed back her chair. "Are you sure?"

"Yes, we won't be but a few minutes."

"All right." Ivy laced her fingers in her lap. What would it be like to have a husband who helped with the dishes? With women's work?

"I see that brain working. Questioning." He winked at her. "Yes, I will help clear the table after dinner and other household chores."

"Life here is so very different. I'm not sure what I expected, but not this. Not a husband who supports and helps his wife. It's refreshing, but…"

"You keep waiting for the other shoe to drop."

"Frankly, yes."

"Well, not all families operate like Nathan and Dinah, but many do. It takes a partnership to run a ranch. The workload is heavy. It should be shared." He cleared his throat. "And speaking of sharing the work, I've spoken to Nathan about hiring one of his Pinkerton colleagues. The agency has resources we don't, and they can investigate this matter in ways we can't."

Tears pricked the backs of her eyes. "But I don't have that kind of money."

"It's my idea, so I'll be footing the bill."

Ivy frowned and crossed her arms. And just like that, the shoe had dropped. He was another man arranging her life. "You didn't talk to me about this first."

"No, we're discussing it now." Confusion etched lines in his forehead. "I don't understand why you're upset. You shouldn't have to be looking over your shoulder in fear that this man or one of his cronies will show up and whisk you back to Pennsylvania. Allen Pinkerton's agents are among the smartest and well-connected people in the country. And they are trained to deal with dangerous individuals like Heisel."

"What if their plan backfires or creates more problems for me?" She leapt from the chair and jabbed her finger at Slade. "He doesn't know where I am. They could lead him right to our door. What were you thinking?"

Nathan came up behind her. "He was thinking that rather than waiting in fear to see if you're discovered, we should be proactive and let the professional solve this problem. It's not going to go away."

She whirled. "You're taking his side?" In her heart, she knew she was overreacting, yet she couldn't tamp down the anger. Their care felt too much like her father's controlling manner. "This is my problem to solve. Not yours. Not his. Mine." She heard the whine in her voice but wouldn't cringe. Wouldn't show vulnerability.

"There are no sides, Ivy," Nathan said. "We want what's best for you…a life without fear."

"Then perhaps it's best that I leave. Find some hole-in-the-wall town that doesn't get one of the city papers. I've put you all in danger. I never should have come." She pushed past Nathan and hurried from the room. Why did she think she could escape her father's machinations?

"Ivy!" Slade's voice followed her up the stairs. His warm, rumbling voice that she'd never wanted to hear again.

Ivy's Inheritance

Chapter Fifteen

The wooden pew bit into the backs of Ivy's legs as she fidgeted and fanned herself. A sigh slipped out, and she clamped her lips together. She sensed Dinah's piercing gaze but didn't glance over to send her an apologetic smile. Despite the open windows in the sanctuary, the room was stifling, seemingly hot enough to roast a turkey. She resisted the urge to tug at her collar and pull it away from her neck. Not that the motion would help. How much longer before summer's heat would leave them?

She blinked and forced herself to focus on Pastor Youst who leaned on the pulpit, wearing a broad smile. A gentle man, he spoke quietly but with authority, his words encouraging and exhorting without judgment.

"So, you see, beloved, God wants what's best for each and every one of you. We must cling to that fact with hope. Not an *I hope Liza at the bakery made coffee cake today*, but a confident expectation knowing that something is going to happen, and you are anticipating it with certainty and assurance."

He pointed to himself and shrugged. "I don't know about you, but sometimes trusting God is difficult for me. Yes, I'm a pastor, but that hardly makes me perfect, and I'm tempted to push my will on to Him. You know, *hoping* He'll keep up." Grinning, Pastor Youst continued, "I don't want to have to go through the fire, and I get angry at God for allowing the difficulties, when instead I should be learning from them and grasping His hand even tighter. He knows my worries. He knows *your* worries."

Ivy pressed a hand to her middle as her stomach hollowed. Was she angry at God for her circumstances? Did she blame Him? Truth be told, she wasn't clinging to Him like the preacher suggested. She'd barely prayed about the situation since concocting the plan with Alma and jumping on the train. She'd been so caught up in fear, she'd taken matters into her own hands. Did God expect her to return to Pennsylvania? Her pulse raced. Surely not.

Pastor Youst's voice broke into her thoughts: "He cares about what distresses you, and He will embrace you as a father cradles his infant. He will also send others to support and help you. Yes, He sometimes intervenes directly, but we are surrounded by other believers, children of God who walk beside us. As it says in the fourth chapter of Ecclesiastes, 'if one prevail against him, two shall withstand him; and a threefold cord is not quickly broken.' We are a family, beloved, and as such we are to be there for each other. To support one another in good times and in bad. To walk beside you during hard times."

He leveled his gaze at the congregation. "Do you find asking for assistance as difficult as I do? Do you feel as if you would be a burden? Are you embarrassed about your circumstances? No matter how long you've been part of our little family, you are welcome, and you are loved. A burden shared is a burden eased."

Out of the corner of her eye, Ivy peered at Slade. The pastor's words struck her deeply. His sermon was so personal. He had to be referring to her when he said no matter how long a person had been there. He had to be speaking about her. How did he know her business? How did he know of her past? As far as anyone, outside of Slade or the Childs, knew, she was simply here as Slade's mail-order bride. Had Slade or Dinah spoken to Pastor Youst about her problem? It was not theirs to share.

She glared at the pastor. How dare he use her as an illustration. Would he never stop talking?

"One last thing, my friends: God is in control. No matter how desperate things seem. The age-old question is why does God allow bad things to happen? Why, indeed? Sometimes, He uses the situation as a time of testing or of growth, but we often don't know why. We cannot see His greater picture."

Ivy swallowed against the nausea that threatened to overtake her. Would God allow Papa's nefarious plan to sell her off in payment of his debts to succeed? Would the Lord allow Mr. Heisel to find her and drag her to the altar, forever binding her to him? Her breath quickened. *Please, God, no.*

Next to her, Slade's form was warm, comforting, and he glanced at her, a concerned expression on his face. She shook her head and gave him what she hoped was a reassuring smile. He was a good man. He'd been nothing but gracious and attentive since her arrival. His offer to marry to ensure her safety seemed genuine and heartfelt, an answer to her problem. He'd assured her the marriage would be in name only until such time as she was ready to be his wife in all sense of the word. She tried to believe him, but no man in her life had proven trustworthy. Men did what they wanted, and women had no say in the matter.

She should at least apologize for last night's outburst in response to his offer to hire a Pinkerton detective. Again, he seemed to have her best interests in mind, but did he really? Perhaps it was in his best interest to be wed. To her or anyone.

Her eyes were drawn to his profile. Square jaw that jutted forward. Later in the day, a shadow would form on his cheeks, tan from hours spent in the sun. His nose just the right size with a slight bump at the bridge. He'd alluded to a story that went with the imperfection but had yet to share. Full lips, and chocolate-brown eyes that missed nothing, always alert, always watching. She could do worse than marrying such a handsome man if marrying was her only choice.

She stilled. Could they pretend to wed? Claim to have married, but not actually go through with the act? Would he agree to such subterfuge? Dare she ask?

Ivy's Inheritance

Chapter Sixteen

Sweat trickled down Slade's back and pooled under his arms as he guided the wagon toward town. The temperature was already stifling and promised another scorcher of a day. A glance at Ivy told him she was suffering as well. Beads of perspiration dotted her upper lip, and her cheeks were flushed. The calendar might say September, but the dog days of August still gripped the plains.

The wagon creaked as it rolled along the rutted dirt lane. Slade's arms rested on his thighs, and the reins lay in his palms. Ned and Ted, the two draft horses, knew the route without any assistance from him, and he let them set their own pace. There was plenty of time before school started, and sitting inches away from Ivy's petite form suited him just fine. She didn't seem to mind the slow pace, either, although the expression on her face said she was miles away. What was she thinking? Hard to say from the look of her, but she seemed content rather than agitated, so perhaps she was simply enjoying the ride.

She asked forgiveness for getting angry about his hiring of a Pinkerton agent, and he assured her he understood, but he knew she wasn't happy about what he'd done. He drank in her profile. Did she have any idea how beautiful she was? Her complexion was smooth and fair, her nose small with a slight upturn. Crystal-blue eyes surveyed the world from under straight brows. A narrow-brimmed hat festooned with a blue ribbon perched on her silky-looking brown hair that was pinned into a bun at the base of her neck. The hat blocked the sun from glinting off the red highlights he'd seen at the church picnic. What would it be like to run his fingers through those tresses?

Pressing his lips together, he swatted away the thought. Vigilant. He must be vigilant. He scanned the fields that flanked the road. Thieves and bandits could easily hide among the cornstalks. Movement on his left, and he jerked his head to get a better look, then blew out his breath. Orville Thacker and a couple of his hands harvesting. Surely, someone looking to snatch Ivy wouldn't be foolish enough to make the attempt with others around to thwart the effort. But the lawless weren't known for their smarts, so he must remain watchful.

Orville waved, and Slade returned the gesture as he spoke. "Did you have a chance to meet Orville Thacker and his wife, Bessie, at the social? They're good people. Salt of the earth."

Ivy nodded. "We didn't have much time together, but they were lovely. And their children quite sweet. Have they been in Lincoln long?"

"A couple of years after the war."

"Seems like many folks did that."

"The idea of a change was appealing to lots of people, especially in the Southern states. Incredible devastation. One hundred and sixty acres free and clear if a person can prove up the land is a tempting offer."

"But hard work."

"Worth every minute and sore muscles." He winked at her. "You're not afraid of hard work, are you?"

She ducked her head. "Of course not. I may have been raised with privileges, but I am willing and able to do what is necessary."

He nudged her shoulder. "I'm teasing. I've seen who you are. You've jumped in with both feet ever since you arrived, helping Dinah, and now, taking on the school. Eventually, you'll stop believing your papa's lies about your lack of worth."

Raising her chin, she met his gaze with tear-filled eyes. Her lips trembled, and he squelched the desire to kiss away her sadness. She'd think him no better than the bounder who'd won her in a card game. He'd have plenty of time for kisses after she agreed to marry him. Would he be able to convince her?

"I'm sor—"

"No need to apologize." Slade frowned. "You've got every right to be struggling. Years of being treated like you were chip away at a person.

But don't forget you're a princess. As one of God's children, you're royalty. After all, He's King."

Her eyes widened. "I never thought of it like that." She giggled. "Do I get a crown, or at least a tiara?"

Chuckling, he said, "I'll see what I can do for you. Do you have a preference of gems?"

Ivy cocked her head and tapped her chin with one finger. "Hmm. I've always been partial to emeralds."

"So noted." He grinned. "Anything else I should know about your particular likes?"

"I'll let you know." A broad smile lit her face, and he was pleased he'd pulled her from the darkness. Even after only a fortnight, he knew he wanted to spend a lifetime making her smile and laugh. If he ever saw that father of hers, he'd be hard-pressed not to punch the man, then ask God's forgiveness afterward.

Minutes elapsed as they rode in companionable silence, passing another farm, then a ranch. Overhead, a hawk swooped and soared in the cloudless sky. Ivy shielded her eyes and watched the bird.

"Guess you didn't have a lot of wildlife in Drexel Hill."

"No, but there are hundreds at the Philadelphia Zoo, the first of its kind in America." Her eyes sparkled with excitement. "It's only been open since seventy-four, even though it was incorporated in 1859. Like everything else, it was delayed by the war. Dr. William Carmac of Philadelphia was inspired after he visited the London Zoo and started campaigning for a zoo years before." She paused. "I imagine you've seen the London Zoo and might not be impressed."

"The London Zoo is remarkable, but that's not to say Philadelphia is less so." He refrained from asking for a tour. She'd be horrified at the thought of returning home, but if he had his way, they'd sweep into Drexel Hill as Mr. and Mrs. Slade Pendleton, heads held high without a worry about the nefarious Gareth Heisel having thwarted his plan. Rogues like him slithered undercover when the light shone on their evil deeds.

The town came into view, and Ivy leaned forward as if willing the wagon to go faster. Slade swallowed a smile and slapped the horses' rumps with the reins. The vehicle picked up speed as the animals cantered along the road, and Ivy sent him a grateful look.

He slowed as they entered the main thoroughfare, then guided the wagon to the lane that led to the school building. He recognized several of the men and women crowding the sidewalks and dipped his head in acknowledgment of their greetings.

Ivy turned toward him. "Do you know everyone in Lincoln?"

"No, but I have been here a while." He jerked his head toward the mercantile. "Do you need to make a stop before we go to school? Now that you've held class, are there items you need? I never met a woman who didn't like to shop."

"Well, you never met me. I don't shop for the sake of shopping. Never have." She frowned. "I have plenty of supplies for now, so you can keep on driving."

"Point taken." He tucked the information into the back of his head. Did she not shop because her father had been stingy, or did she truly not enjoy the activity as a pastime? He appreciated her frugality, but he could afford whatever she wanted. If she gave in and married him, he'd be sure to find out the truth. He'd shower her with gifts if she let him. She deserved nothing less. But first, he'd do everything in his power to keep her safe and out of the clutches of the miscreant in league with her father.

Chapter Seventeen

Ivy nibbled the inside of her cheek. It was a wonder Slade didn't toss her out of the wagon. He'd graciously offered to take her to the store for additional supplies, and she'd bitten off his head. When would she stop being defensive and trust that he had good intentions? After years of living with Papa and being subjected to his machinations, two weeks was not nearly long enough to believe her prospective groom wasn't cut from the same cloth.

She peeked out of the corner of her eye at Slade, then quickly looked away. Gracious, but he was handsome, and if she was reading his posture correctly, he wasn't offended by what she'd said. He sat on the bench, his spine slightly curved with his booted feet propped on the toeboard. The reins rested in his calloused palms as he let the horses take their own pace. His neck swiveled as he watched the scenery pass.

They approached the schoolhouse, and she smiled. Another day teaching the town's children who seemed eager to learn. She'd have to get better at corralling the younger students who fidgeted and whispered among themselves. It might be easier herding cats. She studied the building that had been painted a bright red and trimmed in intricate gingerbread. Who'd had time to carve the woodwork? Someone as excited as her about school. A small stoop and a set of double doors created a welcoming entrance.

"You're wiggling like a toddler on Christmas Eve." Slade chuckled. "I don't recall any of my teachers seeming as delighted as you."

"Then shame on them." Ivy shook her head. "Nothing is more exciting them opening young minds to possibilities. To prepare them with skills that will carry them through life."

He looked at her with a mixture of admiration and an emotion she couldn't read, and her cheeks warmed. Perhaps she'd been a little too vehement in her opinion.

Nodding, he said, "You're right."

Her shoulders sagged. Once again, she'd been sharp with him, and he hadn't reprimanded her sassiness.

"Whoa." Slade pulled back on the reins, and the wagon rolled to a stop. He set the brake. "Stay there, and I'll help you down. Can't let that pretty dress get soiled."

He jumped to the ground, then looped the traces around the hitching post. Patting each horse, he spoke quietly to them. A small act, but the animals didn't lie. If he treated them poorly, they'd be skittish or mean, and both were gentle giants. More proof of Slade's good character?

Finished conversing with the animals, he made his way to her side of the wagon. Winking, he said, "Must thank the lads for their hard work in getting us here."

Ivy's cheeks heated for the second time since she'd climbed into the wagon. Since when did a wink and a few kind words send her pulse tripping? She needed to get a better grip on her emotions. Standing, she smoothed her skirts as Slade held up his hand. She gripped his warm fingers, then stepped on top of the wheel, and her petticoat got caught under her shoe. Teetering, she tugged at the fabric and shifted her foot in an effort to free herself. Bad choice. She pitched forward.

With a grunt she crashed into Slade's broad chest, and his arm wrapped around her waist preventing her from falling in a heap. Her face flamed with embarrassment as she stared into his chocolate-brown eyes inches from hers. His pupils dilated, and his gaze slid to her mouth. His heart pounded against hers through the thin fabric of her dress. He slowly lowered her until her feet touched the ground, but he continued to hold her, staring as if he'd never seen her before.

A shiver snaked up her spine as time seemed to stand still. His grip tightened, and he dipped his head to brush his lips against her. Gently, softly. She sighed, and he pressed his lips more firmly against hers, becoming more insistent, searching. Tingles shot from her mouth, down her neck, into her arms, and out through her fingertips. She melted against him returning his kiss.

He broke free and pushed his hat back on his head. "I'm sorry. I shouldn't have taken such liberties. You must think me a terrible bounder. Kissing you in public. Kissing you at all."

She wrapped her arms around her middle and locked her knees to keep from falling to the ground. She read cheap novels about women swooning after being kissed by the hero which she'd thought was utter claptrap. Until today. Her body had responded in ways she'd never imagined, and swooning was a definite possibility. "Um, there's no need to apologize."

"It won't happen again." His body stiff, he motioned to the schoolhouse. "Let's get you inside. The children will be here shortly."

Nodding, she lifted her skirts to prevent another incident, then walked past him and into the building. Sunlight poured through the windows and puddled onto the floor. The thud of Slade's footsteps sounded behind her. How would she get through an entire day of teaching in his presence?

As if he could read her thoughts, he said, "I can stand guard outside, if that would make you more comfortable."

"Nonsense." Ivy shook her head. "After all, I came out here as your mail-order bride-to-be. You have every right to kiss me."

"I'm not that kind of man. I will not force myself on you." He removed his hat and clenched the brim in his hands. "I do want you to marry me, but it will be a marriage in name only until you're ready. Until you care enough about me to consummate the relationship."

"We can't marry. I never should have agreed to come. The Bible says a child must honor their father and mother. I should have remained and done as Papa asked. Instead, I've put you in danger."

He strode toward her, his face a thunderous mask as he tossed his hat on the desk. "God does not expect you to marry a man to get your father out of debt because of his gambling habit. Shame on him for demanding it of you. And I'm not worried about the danger. You may not want to marry me, but I will keep you safe. You've not said much about the man, but I've seen his kind before. He's cruel and manipulative and probably abusive, verbally if not physically." He ran his thumb against her jaw, then tucked a stray hair behind her ear. "I've promised to protect you, and I will whether or not we wed, but I do hope you'll consider marrying me. I've grown to care about you. Quite a bit. And I think you're beginning to care for me as well. You kissed me back."

Would her face never return to its normal shade? Yes, she'd returned his kiss, but foolishly, she hoped he hadn't noticed. So much for that wish.

Slade cradled her hands in his. "Please marry me, Ivy, and make me the happiest man on earth."

Desire and doubt warred within her as she searched his face. He'd treated her kindly. No, more than kindly. He was generous and gracious. Solicitous and sensitive, yet manly. A razor-sharp wit that made her laugh.

Intelligent with eyes that missed nothing. And she'd seen his capabilities with a gun. He certainly had the skills to protect her, but would it come to that? Would Mr. Heisel hunt her down as if he were on safari, and she was the trophy? Would marrying Slade truly make all her troubles disappear? "I-I need more time."

His face fell, and he released her hands. "I understand. I'll be outside if you need me." He turned on his heel, grabbed his hat, and walked to the door.

"Slade!"

He turned, his expression expectant.

"I'm sorry." Her hands fluttered. "We have two more weeks. I won't make you wait longer than that."

"Fair enough. But it might be too late by then." He slipped out the door, and it closed with a quiet thud.

Her eyes welled with tears, and she blinked them away. She'd hurt him. Badly. He'd bared himself to her, and she rejected him. She raised her gaze to the ceiling. "Dear God, tell me what to do."

The door burst open, and her students raced into the room, giggling and shouting. She smiled at their enthusiasm. "Thank You, Father. One step at a time. Teaching the children, then deciding how to get out of this mess."

Chapter Eighteen

Slade strode down the wooden sidewalk in town, shouldering his way through the crowds. Two days had passed since he'd asked Ivy to marry him. Not asked. Begged. She must think him a poor excuse for a husband. Why else would she ask for more time? She was probably hoping for a better offer. He growled, and the woman approaching him widened her eyes and pressed close to the buildings, her reticule clutched to her chest. Touching the brim of his hat, he sent her an apologetic smile.

Great, now he was scaring the female population. A sigh slipped out, and he turned down the street that led to the newly formed park. A gazebo stood in the middle of the grassy expanse and had already been used several times for concerts and lectures. Trees had been brought in to provide shade, but a few years would have to elapse before any real protection would be available. A handful of benches were parked under the saplings, and he made his way the nearest one. Unable to keep his mind on ranch chores, he'd offered to come to town to do the banking and pick up mail and supplies. But if the poor woman on the street was any indication, he needed to get a grip on his emotions before entering any of the establishments.

He sat down, laced his fingers, and stared at the ground. Movement caught his eye, and he watched a cricket crawl through the tangled grass moving one way, then another as it encountered an area too thick to push through. "Did You just send me a message, Lord? Are you telling me to persevere with Ivy? Will she ultimately choose me if I prove myself reliable and honorable? I know she struggles with trust. I cannot be forceful with her as her father was, circumventing her will with mine."

Slade took off his hat, set it on the bench, and ran his fingers through his hair. He felt a little foolish praying out loud, but his mind wandered sometimes when he prayed silently, and this was an important issue. One, he had to get right, and to do that he needed a serious conversation with his heavenly Father.

Closing his eyes, Slade shut out the world. "Lord, I know You are in control. You know exactly what is going to happen, and whatever that is will be Your perfect plan. Help me not to bungle things with Ivy. She doesn't realize how much danger she is in. Men like Heisel will do despicable things to get their own way. They don't like to be made fools of, and like a cornered wild animal are mean and unpredictable. Please protect her, Father, and tell me how to keep her safe, too. She is so very special, and yet, she doesn't see her worth. Help her learn that, as one of Your creations, she is unique and of value."

A breeze wafted past Slade, ruffling his hair and stroking his cheeks. He smiled. "I'm going to believe that's You, Lord. Thanks for the confirmation of Your presence and Your care. I don't have the answers yet, but I know You'll inform me when the time is right. And unless I hear differently from You, I'm going to marry that girl and spend the rest of my life making her feel loved and cherished."

Feeling lighter than he had since Ivy had arrived, Slade jumped to his feet. He'd been trying to fix things on his own, sending an occasional prayer upward. He knew better than to approach a battle unprepared. Especially a spiritual battle, which is exactly what was happening. The man determined to marry Ivy was evil, and like Paul said in the Bible, Slade needed to be fully clothed in the armor of God. He wasn't sure where it said prayer was part of the armor, and he'd look it up later, but right now, he'd pray with every breath until victorious. God's victory, not his.

He clamped his hat on his head and retraced his steps. A young couple strolled along the path leading to the gazebo, and he smiled widely as he doffed his hat. They nodded at him, then exchanged a loving glance. How soon before he would be sauntering arm in arm with sweet Ivy? An image of her heart-shaped face and smooth ivory complexion floated into his mind, and he increased his pace. First to the bank and post office, then the mercantile to see if he had a report from the Pinkerton agent. He'd gone against Ivy's wishes and hired the man. Slade would add it to the list of actions she'd need to forgive him for.

His boots clomped on the sidewalk as he hurried to complete his errands: first the bank to retrieve cash for payroll, then to the post office for any mail the men might have received. Fifteen minutes later, he entered the mercantile, the bell on the door announcing his presence.

Luther waved at him from behind the counter, the beefy man the size of a grizzly but with the heart of kitten. He never met a stranger and often gave items to folks in town who were in a financial bind. He never made a big deal of it, and as far as Slade knew only the pastor and he were aware of Luther's generosity. "Any new items that might be of interest?"

"Well, if you're a reader, I got in a shipment of books. Some of them published this year, and a couple by your countrymen, Henry James and Thomas Hardy." He snapped his fingers, then slipped from behind the counter and hurried to a nearby shelf where he selected one of the volumes. "You might like this one. A detective story that has hit the US by storm. A woman, if you can imagine it, has written a mystery story called *The Leavenworth Case*. Quite a thrilling story, if you ask me."

A vision of sitting on the sofa and reading aloud to Ivy flashed through Slade's mind, and he reached for the book. "I'll take all three, thank you. Put them on my account." He surveyed the shop. "Anything else?"

"Clothing and boots as well as some sewing items."

Slade pulled a list from his shirt pocket. "I'm set with those but need a few supplies for the ranch. Also, I'm waiting for a telegram."

Luther rolled his eyes. "*Ach du Lieber*, how could I forget? My apologies."

"It's my fault." Slade chuckled. "I distracted you by asking about new products, and books are your favorite topic."

"*Ja*, they are at that." Luther grinned, walked behind the counter and laid down the books, then bent and rummaged underneath. "Here it is." His voice was muffled as his hand appeared, clutching a small envelope. He gave it to Slade, then scribbled the date and time in his ledger and turned the book for Slade to sign. He took the list. "It won't take me long to pull these items together if you have other errands in town."

Slade tucked the telegram into his pocket. He'd read it when he was alone, then come back and send a reply if necessary. "No, that's it, and I'll take care of loading the wagon if you'll handle the paperwork."

"Ja, gut."

A half hour later, Slade sat in the heavily packed wagon as it rolled out of town. Once again, he gave the horses their head and pulled out the cable. He slit the envelope, then withdrew the small page. Scanning the words quickly, he frowned. The reprobate not only wouldn't take money or goods to go away, but he'd threatened Ivy's friend and her family to tell him where Ivy had gone. Unfortunately, before the family's butler had surprised everyone by knocking out the man with one punch, then calling the authorities after tying him up, Ivy's friend gave him the name of the matrimonial agency. Heisel sweet-talked and paid his way out of jail before disappearing, ostensibly to find Mrs. Crenshaw. The agent had warned the widow, but she'd assured him she was quite safe, always keeping a bodyguard on hand. Was the mail-order bride business that dangerous?

    Slade frowned and rubbed his forehead, then shoved the cable back into the envelope and returned it to his pocket. "All right, Lord, I'm all ears for whatever You've got planned."

Chapter Nineteen

Ivy flicked her gaze at the large clock over the doorway and huffed out a sigh. Finally, time to dismiss class, and not a minute too soon. The children had been alternately rambunctious and sullen, with every assignment being a battle. What had gotten into them? There were no holidays forthcoming or special events she was aware of. Perhaps they simply had a bad case of cabin fever. She'd given them extra time at recess, but the break had done little to change their behavior.

She clapped her hands. "I expect better things from you all tomorrow, but you are dismissed."

A loud cheer filled the room as the students clambered from their chairs, then raced for the door, footsteps pounding. She didn't bother to correct them as she doubted they'd hear her voice over the ruckus. Was she in over her head? Why was she not able to control a group of children?

She'd have to give her tactics deep thought tonight. How could she make learning enjoyable, but still keep some semblance of order in the room?

Sighing, she brushed a stray hair from her face, then turned and picked up the cloth to erase the board. Shoulders aching, she rubbed at the chalk until the marks disappeared. Slate clean, she straightened the books and papers on her desk, then lowered herself into the chair and bowed her head. "Dear God, I need Your help. The students are getting the best of me, and I don't know what to do. I thought teaching would be easy, and it is anything but. How can I capture the students' desire for learning? I loved school. I don't understand their reticence. Granted, their background is so very different than mine. They must rise before dawn and complete chores before coming. That was not my lot in life. Please guide me."

Meet them where they are.

Warmth like a quilt enveloped her. "Lord?"

Meet them where they are.

A smile broke out on her face. In all her years of believing in God, she'd never heard Him speak to her. Or did she imagine His voice? Either way, He gave her what she needed.

The poor dears went from chores to schoolwork. She'd start the day by giving them a fifteen-minute recess where they could be children and have fun. Then she'd have the older students help the younger ones. Not the whole time, but for segments of the day. And she'd intersperse activities with book learning, plus only use thirty minutes for each subject.

They wouldn't cover all topics every day. Perhaps that would make them look forward to them.

Her heart pounded as she grabbed a sheet of paper and pencil, then scribbled notes about a schedule for the next few days. Discouragement gone, she could hardly keep up with the ideas that flowed like a waterfall.

"Aren't you a busy one?"

Ivy jerked up her head as she dropped the pencil. Her heard pounded. "Slade! I didn't hear you come in."

A crooked smile bloomed on his face. "That's obvious. You look a bit like the mad scientist hunched over your paper writing as if your life depended on it. I hated to break your concentration, but we need to get a move on if we're not going to be late for dinner at Dinah's."

"Of course." She pulled her reticule from the desk drawer and tucked the paper inside, then tied on her bonnet. "I was so engrossed I forgot you were outside."

He chuckled. "See? I said you'd get used to me guarding you." He motioned toward the door. "Shall we?"

She walked down the aisle aware of his closeness behind her. Of his strength and confidence, not arrogance like Papa. She stepped outside and took a deep breath. The clean Nebraska air filled her lungs as she admired the sweeping blue expanse of the sky. "I'll never tire of the beauty here," Ivy said as she descended the stairs, then braced herself for the feel of his fingers on hers.

Slade helped her into the wagon. She sat down, then tucked her hands under her thighs. As was his habit, he spoke to the horses, then climbed onto the buckboard. He slapped the reins, and the conveyance jerked forward. "I've got news."

"News?" Her pulse thrummed. "Good or bad?"

He pulled a telegram from his shirt pocket and handed it to her. "Read this, then we'll talk."

She unfolded the cable, and her gaze raced down the page. Emotions warred within her. Anger that Slade had taken matters into his own hands after she asked him not to seek help from the Pinkertons and relief that someone in authority knew what was going on. She slumped on the bench still gripping the missive. She was tired of being afraid. Tired of feeling guilty that Slade was putting his ranch duties aside to guard her. And she didn't want to start over anywhere else. She'd grown to love the town and its people in the short time since she'd arrived.

Most of all, she'd begun to care for Slade. She looked forward to seeing him each morning, and he was the last thing she thought about before falling asleep. He was not like the other men in her life.

"What's going on inside that head of yours?" He nudged her shoulder. "You were upset, but now you seem…resigned. I'm sorry I went against your wishes, but I only did it to keep you safe."

"I know." She nodded. "I've been managing on my own for so long, I'm not good at accepting help. Especially from men."

"Understandable. Your experiences have taught you that most, if not all of us, can't be trusted. I hope you realize I'm not like that."

She nodded as she swallowed the lump that had formed in her throat. He was a good man.

"I, um, hadn't planned to do this again, at least not yet, and certainly not during a wagon ride, but it seems like you might be amenable to the idea. Will you marry me, Ivy? Not because it will keep you out of Gareth Heisel's clutches, but because I care about you. More than any woman I've ever known. It would be a marriage in name only, until you said differently."

Ivy licked her lips. Is this what God had planned all along?

Slade held his breath as he waited for her answer. He'd rambled on like a simpleton all the while watching emotions flit across her face. Had he put his foot in it again?

"Yes, I'll marry you." Ivy sent him a dazzling smile. "I've begun to care for you, too."

"You will? That's wonderful!" He pulled on the reins. The horses stopped, and he set the brake, then wrapped his arms around her. "Thank you. I'm not perfect, but I'll work to be the best husband a woman ever had."

She laughed into his shoulder and said in a muffled voice, "I'm not perfect, either, but we'll figure it out."

He let her go, grinning like a child on Christmas morning. He released the brake and got the wagon moving again. "I can't wait to tell Nathan and Dinah."

Laying a hand on his arm, she said, "May I have some time to plan the wedding?"

"Of course, no bride should have to rush the blessed event, but considering the circumstances, can you be ready in a week? I know that's soon, but Dinah will commandeer the women at church, and you'll have the wedding of the century. No disrespect intended, but they'll work a miracle that rivals Jesus' fish and loaves."

Giggling, she said, "The ladies at my church were the same way. A force to be reckoned with. Let's make it nine days. Today is Thursday, and I'd rather not get married on a school day."

"I should have thought of that. I guess I'm a bit anxious."

Slade squelched the desire to lace his fingers with hers or wrap one arm around her shoulder. He needed both hands to drive even though the horses knew their way to the Childs's ranch. Plus, there were two spots along the way that could easily hide someone intent on ambush. Not that he'd tell Ivy. He slid his gaze toward her and sent a grateful prayer heavenward that she'd agreed to be his wife. He was the most blessed man in all of Lincoln.

He'd told her the marriage would be in name only, but she'd said she cared for him, too. Would he have long to wait before he could show her how much he loved her? He blinked. Did he love her? The word entered his mind unbidden. Had the Lord put it there? Was it his own realization? Despite his *advanced* age, his knowledge of love would fit on the head of a pin. Leaving England, then fighting in the war had prevented any courting. Then he'd moved to the West and focused on his ranch.

What he did know was that he would give his very life to protect this precious woman. He couldn't wait to see her each morning and missed her desperately when he left her in the care of Nathan and Dinah. She made him laugh with her wry sense of humor, and her intelligence allowed her to converse on any topic. Her faith made her as beautiful on the inside as she was on the outside. He'd never grow tired of looking at her.

And perhaps she'd eventually love him as well. A man could hope. But no matter what, marrying her would make her safe. Problem solved.

The hair on the back of his neck prickled, and he straightened his spine as he surveyed the fields on either side of the road. His eyes strained to look among the cornstalks for any suspicious movement. The problem wasn't solved yet, and he'd allowed his joy at her acceptance to lower his guard. Fortunately, he'd come his senses. *If that's You, Lord, I appreciate the assistance.*

Slade slapped the reins, urging the horses into a canter as he forced a smile and said, "I'm hungrier than I thought, and we've got news to share." *And keep us safe until we get there, Father.*

Ivy's Inheritance

Chapter Twenty

Slade cast a glance at the sky and grinned as he followed the fence that bordered the ranch. He'd been riding for a couple of hours, but the time had passed in a blink as he ruminated over the last forty-eight hours. What a difference two days made. The overhead expanse seemed bluer, and the sun seemed to shine brighter. Birds chirped louder and danced on the thermals. All because Ivy had agreed to marry him. Only seven days remained until the blessed event.

A short distance away two of the hands were repairing the fence, and they waved as he approached. "How goes it, gents? This is one of the more tedious jobs."

The smaller of the two, a wiry young man in his early twenties shrugged. "We're outside, and the weather is fine. May as well be doing this as something else."

"I like your attitude." Slade nodded at him.

His face flushed, deepening his tanned cheeks. "Truth be told, I was complaining earlier, and Monty, um, reminded me that we have it good here, sir."

Monty grinned and pushed his hat back on his head. "Sometimes you've gotta lay it out for these young-uns. How goes it with you, Slade? Bet you're strugglin' to concentrate on account of gettin' married. Congratulations."

"Thanks, and you're right." Slade straightened in the saddle. "I was helping with weighing the calves, but the lads told me I was slowing them down." He chuckled. "Who talks to their boss like that?"

"Men who are treated like equals." Monty laughed. "That's what you get for being a good leader."

Slade's chest lightened. Monty had been cowboying for longer than Slade had been alive. The man's opinion meant a lot because he'd seen a lot. "Enough buttering up the boss. I'll let you get back to business."

The pair nodded and bent over the upright as Slade kneed the horse into motion. A light breeze stroked his cheeks as he squinted to survey his land. A few more weeks, and the men would turn their hand toward harvesting, but for now it was all about preparing for winter. Weeding pastures, gathering hay and feed, maintaining the equipment, and determining which cattle would remain for next season and which would be sold. Weighing the animals and checking the pregnancy status of the heifers was part of that decision. The vet would be by to check their health, too.

He continued riding, and an hour passed, then two. His stomach rumbled reminding him that breakfast was a distant memory, and he'd eaten before sunup. The sound of clanging wafted toward him. Lunch was being served at the bunkhouse. Excellent. He could leave the beef jerky in his saddlebag for another time. Leaning forward, he yelled, "Hyah," and Midnight surged forward, mane flying.

The animal's hooves thundered across the hard ground as they ate up the acres. Slade gripped the reins as Midnight galloped toward the homestead, muscles bunching. His favorite horse loved speed, as did Slade. The two were a matched pair. As they got closer to the barn, Midnight slowed to a cantor, then a walk, and Slade grinned. Yes, sir. Midnight was the smartest horse he'd ever owned. It was as if the beast could read his mind.

In front of the massive barn, they came to a stop, and Slade slid to the ground. Midnight nickered and bobbed his head as if to say thank you for letting him stretch his legs. "Good boy. Let's get you brushed down and watered. An extra rasher of oats, too."

Slade led him into the dim recesses of the barn and unbuckled the flank cinch and breast collar. After undoing the girth, he brought the clip up to the D-ring on the breast collar, then grabbed the saddle horn and pad and pulled the saddle from Midnight's back. He hung the saddle over one of the wooden racks and stroked the burnished leather. The seat had seen him through the war and beyond. He secured Midnight's bridle to a hook on the wall in preparation for brushing him down.

Footsteps sounded behind him, and he turned. A lanky, unshaven man in chaps and smelling strongly of sweat strolled toward him. He didn't recognize the cowboy from any of the nearby ranches. Was he a stranger in town? Unless he'd been fired, the man should still be working. Everyone needed a full bunkhouse this time of year. There were plenty of tasks to be done before winter. "May I help you?" Acting casual, Slade hung the tack on the wall, then moved his right hand to his hip where his revolver rested in the holster.

The man yanked the worn and battered Stetson from his head and clutched it in both hands. His eyes shifted right, then left, then back again. "Yes, sir. I'm, um, lookin' for work, and a couple of your boys said you might be hiring."

Slade's gut tightened. The man hadn't said or done anything wrong, but something was telling him to be careful. "What's your name? Where'd you come from?"

"Will Hoyle. The Bar J over in Emerald."

"That right?" Slade cocked his head. "Why didn't they need you? This is a busy time for ranchers."

"Yes, sir, but the owner, Mr. Jameson, died, and his widow sold off everything to head back East. New owner brought in his own men."

"Emerald's a hike from here. No one is hiring between there and here?" Something was off about the man, and Slade would find out what.

He could send a telegram to Emerald easy enough, but a response might take a couple of days.

"No, sir." His eyes shifted again. "Seems everybody has all the help they need."

"What are you good at? I need lads who can do anything I ask."

Hoyle shrugged. "Just about anything. I've broken horses, mended fences, harvested crops, branded. You name it, I can do it. I just need a place to hang my hat."

Slade studied the man for a long moment, and instead of looking down, Hoyle met his gaze. Was the man's initial shiftiness simply a case of nerves? Which persona was the real cowboy? "All right, Hoyle, I'll give you a chance, but if I think you're being underhanded in any way, I'll send you packing. Understood?"

"Yes, sir." Hoyle's smile was wide with a gap on one side where he'd lost two teeth. "I won't let you down, sir. I can start right away."

"Fair enough." Slade motioned to Midnight. "Let's see how you brush down my favorite horse, and I'll give you the rules of the ranch."

"He's a mighty fine horse, sir. I can see why he's your favorite." Hoyle plunked his hat back on his head. "Where do you keep the combs and brushes, sir?"

Slade pointed to the items on a nearby bench. Hoyle grabbed a curry comb and using short circular motions, loosened dirt and hair from the horse. Satisfied the man knew what he was doing, Slade leaned against the wall. "Honesty will cover a multitude of sins, Hoyle. There's no harm in making mistakes, but if you lie to cover it up, I'll show you the door. We work hard, but I pay a good wage." He named a figure, then continued, "I won't abide drinking, swearing, or smoking. I'm a God-fearing man, and I won't have any of those things on my ranch. You don't have to believe like I do, but I expect your behaviors to be above reproach. Most of all, I'm getting married next Saturday, and when my bride comes to live here, you're to give her a wide berth unless she seeks you out for assistance. If she does need help, you're to treat her with the utmost respect." Slade narrowed his eyes. "Any of this going to be a problem for you, Hoyle?"

"No, sir. Not at all." Hoyle changed out the curry comb for a stiff brush and with short, firm strokes at Midnight's neck, removed more flecks of mud. "I don't want no trouble."

"You're hired, but I'll be watching you closely." Slade held out his hand, and Hoyle shook it with a firm grip. Was the man a down-and-out cowboy as he appeared, or would he give French actress Sarah Bernhardt a run for her money on the stage? Time would tell. Meanwhile, he'd pair Monty with the man. If anyone could ferret out the truth, it was the grizzled cowhand. "When you're finished there, lunch is being served in the bunkhouse. Come over, and I'll introduce you to the others and set you up with a bed."

"Yes, sir. Thank you, sir. You won't regret this."

"See that I don't." Slade strode from the barn, already regretting the decision, but he wasn't one to go back on his word.

Chapter Twenty-One

Eyes welling, Ivy studied herself in the mirror, fingering the teal fabric, then raised her eyes and met Dinah's gaze. "I can't believe you altered this dress in four days. It's gorgeous."

Grinning, Dinah shook her head. "The church ladies and I have been working on this since you arrived in town, and we saw that you were similar in size to Pansy Horton. She happily contributed the dress. It was given to her when she married."

"Since I arrived?" Ivy gaped at her friend, then giggled. "How optimistic. I wasn't sure I was even staying."

"Mrs. Crenshaw is never wrong."

"Apparently." Ivy shrugged. "Anyway, passing down the wedding is a lovely tradition. I look forward to handing it down to the next bride."

"But first we get you married." Dinah poked her. "Now, sit so I can practice doing your hair."

Ivy plopped into the chair they'd dragged in from the kitchen, and her stomach tightened. "It's been a while since I've had a lady's maid. Within a year of Mama's death, Papa started gambling, and he had to let several staff go when the finances took a, um, downturn."

Dinah picked up a brush from the dresser, then grinned at Ivy in the reflection. "Well, I could come to the ranch every morning, if you'd like."

"As much as I'd enjoy that, I'm sure Nathan would have something to say about it." Ivy laughed. God had blessed her with Dinah's friendship, and a fresh start. Dredging up old memories didn't do her any good. "Maybe only on Sundays."

Snorting a laugh, Dinah began brushing Ivy's long strands.

Closing her eyes, Ivy sagged against the chair as the rhythmic strokes on her scalp drained the tension from the rest of her body. She'd try not to think about the fact that it should be Mama brushing her hair, or at least sitting on the bed keeping her company as she prepared her on her wedding day. Alma, too. What was her friend doing?

Fall would have started, with cooler temperatures and the foliage turning shades of yellow, orange, and red as if God had swiped His paintbrush along the edge of each leaf. The sky would be a brilliant shade of blue, like the tiny robin's eggs she saw each spring in the nest outside the kitchen. Puffy white clouds would play cat and mouse with the sun.

Nebraska had its own beauty, but she would miss the trees and rolling hills of Pennsylvania.

Only three weeks had elapsed since she'd pulled out of the train station in Philadelphia, yet it seemed like a lifetime.

Ivy plucked at her skirts, but kept her eyes closed. "Dinah, what was it like for you? How did you know marrying Nathan was the right thing to do?"

"I haven't told you my story, but I think it's time." Dinah squeezed Ivy's shoulder, then continued to pin up her hair. "I also came West to escape a bad family situation. My brothers were part of a violent gang in Baltimore. It was awful. They did terrible things. When I arrived, I realized they were responsible for the death of Nathan's first wife, they set fire to a building she was in while visiting Maryland."

Ivy gasped, and her eyes flew open. "No!"

"Yes." Dinah nodded as she sighed. "And like yours, my father had a gambling addiction that affected our finances. Badly. I tried to find work to help bring in money, but with my family, um, *connections*, no one would hire me. Then I was attacked by a man whose brother was crippled by my brother during a bank robbery. That's when I realized Baltimore was no longer safe for me. I had no choice but to apply as a bride."

She laid down the brush and faced Ivy. "God intervened immediately. The deputy who saved me during the attack took me to the hotel across the street. He knew about my family and that I was not involved in their activities. He suggested I leave town and consider becoming a mail-order bride. Mrs. Crenshaw was in the lobby and overheard the conversation. She had just received Nathan's letter asking for a wife."

Heart pounding, Ivy reached for Dinah's hands. "Did you tell Nathan about your brother's role in his wife's death?"

"No, he found out from Sheriff Denard. Needless to say, he was upset...angry that I hadn't told him. But before we could talk about the situation, we discovered that his daughter, Florence, had been kidnapped."

"How frightening!"

"You have no idea." Dinah gave her a tremulous smile. "But God allowed us to find her and bring the kidnappers to justice. Eventually, things worked out between us, but not without a lot of conversation and even more prayer. Prayer is the key, Ivy. I believe with all my heart that God intervened for you, too. That He provided Mrs. Crenshaw's agency and Slade, but your marriage won't succeed without prayer and a commitment to make it work." She enveloped Ivy in a warm hug, then released her and picked up the brush. "Now, enough about me. This time is about you, and I've only managed to get half your hair done. Not the look you want."

Ivy giggled, then sobered. "Thanks for sharing your story. It means a lot that you would tell me. You understand, like none of the others. I do want my marriage to work, but I feel so ill-prepared."

"As do most couples when they're starting out. You'll learn as you go. Mistakes and arguments will happen, but nothing is irreparable with

God in the partnership." Dinah laughed. "And I'm always available for a nickel's worth of free advice."

"I'll be sure to keep coins on hand."

Slade removed his hat and blotted the perspiration on his face with his handkerchief. The days had finally begun to cool, but wrestling five-hundred-pound calves to the ground to be branded worked up a sweat. They'd finished a short time ago, and he decided to check on the new hand. According to Monty, the man had been quiet most of the evening last night, keeping to himself. Not a bad thing at face value, and perhaps he was simply shy, but Slade wouldn't rest easy until he got word back from the Bar J. Hopefully, his concerns were for naught.

This morning, he'd started the man out easy, mending fences with Monty and one of the other newer lads. Monty was as clever as an undercover Pinkerton agent in ferreting out information. He'd yammer on, playing the part of the harmless, aging cowboy, all the while watching for reactions and drawing the individual into a conversation or an argument if he could. Monty claimed he got more information out of a frustrated guy.

That's how they'd discovered a cattle rustler who was trying to infiltrate Slade's operation. Monty had waffled on for three days about how smart he was until the boy finally pulled his weapon and blurted out that if Monty had any kind of brains, he'd recognize a thief when he saw one. Laughing, the old hand told him he'd known all along, and that he'd emptied the lad's gun. Slade still remembered the look on the rustler's face when Monty brought him back to the house wrapped up like a Christmas present and strapped to his horse. Hopefully, a couple of years in jail would teach the young man that stealing wasn't worth the punishment. Unfortunately, some people never learned.

Slade wandered to the barn and saddled Midnight, then climbed onto the animal and headed toward the far pastures. The earthy odor of manure and cows wafted toward him on the breeze. Pungent, yet less off-putting than the street smells of London. Some days he missed the conveniences of living in a city where everything he could possibly need was close by, but most days he was thrilled to have started this new chapter. He'd never quite fit into his father's world of rule-filled polite society. No, his heart was in America. A country where a man could arrive with little more than his clothes and a dream and become a wealthy ranch owner. A country where each man could have his own opinion and way of doing things.

Midnight squealed, then sidestepped, yanking Slade from his musings, nearly unseating him. "Whoa, Midnight, what is it?" Slade pulled out his pistol and raked the ground with his eyes. A rattle and hiss drew his gaze to the snake coiled a few feet away. In a flash, he shot the rattler, and silence fell. Whinnying, the horse pranced, then settled as Slade patted his neck. "Easy, Midnight. You're all right now."

Heart pounding, Slade blew out a loud breath. Not paying attention could get a man killed. *Thank You, Lord, for watching over me.* Another couple of breaths, then he kneed Midnight into motion, and they continued making their way to the far end of the ranch. He'd like to have approached Monty and the lads without notice, but Nebraska's lack of forestry made that an impossibility. He should have brought a pair of field glasses, but it was too late now.

He pinned on a smile and urged the horse into a cantor. The men looked up as he approached, their expressions an interesting mixture. From beside the wagon, Monty shot him a self-satisfied smile seeming to say he'd delved into Hoyle's history. On his knees near one of the fence posts, Hoyle looked nervous, and Corey curious. Nervous was normal, but twenty-four hours was not enough time to make a final judgment about the man's honesty and intentions. Especially, knowing Ivy's papa and the fiend he'd sold her to would do anything to get their hands on her.

Monty had asked Slade why he was willing to bring on the new man considering the danger to Ivy, and he'd replied that keeping Hoyle where he could see him could be safer. Hopefully, the decision would prove to be the right one.

"Carry on, gents; just swinging by to see how things are going. Mending fences is a tedious job."

Monty straightened and jerked his head toward the two hands. "They work well together. We've made good time and should be finished before suppertime."

"Excellent." Slade glanced at the men who'd risen and stood stiffly near the fence. "Good work, lads. With the wedding in three days' time, it's important to get ahead of the chores."

Hoyle squinted at him. "When you took me on, I didn't realize the weddin' was so soon. Congratulations, sir."

Slade gave him a long look trying to read the man but got nothing. "Thank you. You're all invited, of course."

"Thank you, sir, but somebody's gotta watch the ranch, don't they? I can do that."

"All by yourself, lad?"

Red blotches worked their way up from Hoyle's neck to his face, and he dragged off his hat. "Well, no, sir, but I could be one of the sentries."

"You expecting trouble?" Slade raised one eyebrow. "You know something I don't?"

"What? No, sir." The young man shrugged. "Maybe I'm out of line, but I just never seen a ranch left unattended. There's always someone on the property. I'm offerin' 'cause I'm the new guy."

"Thanks. I'll let you know." Slade exchanged a glance with Monty, then touched the brim of his hat. "Carry on."

He wheeled the horse around and retraced their steps toward the house. Little did the kid know, the last thing Slade would do was leave him at the ranch out of sight. Hopefully, concerns about the lad would prove unfounded, but Slade's gut told him differently.

Chapter Twenty-Two

Waving at the ranch hand who lounged against the small pile of boulders about fifty yards from the schoolhouse, Ivy climbed the steps, then paused on the porch and surveyed the grassy expanse. The hair on the back of her neck had prickled the entire time she and the children were outside, but she'd seen nothing out of the ordinary. Anyone approaching down the lane from town would be seen, and surely the cornfields behind the building were too far away to create danger. She ducked inside the building behind the students. Slade told her last night he wouldn't be on guard today, but that didn't assuage the disappointment lodged in her chest or the feeling that she was safer under his eagle eye rather than one of the men.

Thumps and bumps filled the room as the children found their places on the benches. She leaned against her desk and smiled as they looked up, expectancy written on their faces. Her heart swelled. She'd had no idea teaching would be so fulfilling when she'd agreed to take the job. It had seemed a means to an end, yet opening the children's eyes to the mysteries of numbers and words brought her unexpected joy.

"Welcome, everyone! Thank you for coming. I thought we'd start our morning by beginning a new book."

A couple of the boys who struggled with reading groaned, but the rest of the kids perked up.

She picked up two volumes from her desk. "The best way to get better is to practice, so we will all take turns, but first, let's choose which book we'd like. *The Adventures of Tom Sawyer* by Mark Twain. It's a very fun story about a boy who is the age of many of you, although he often plays hooky, which I do not condone." She grinned to take the sting from her words. "The other book is by an Englishman, a mathematics teacher at one of the great universities in England, and it's called *Alice's Adventures in Wonderland*. She falls down a rabbit hole and meets all sorts of unusual creatures."

"Alice!"

"Tom!"

"Alice!"

Ivy let the excited chatter continue for a moment, her heart full at the children's eagerness, then laid down the books and clapped her hands. Silence fell. "Raise your hand for Tom." Arms shot up, and she counted.

"Now, raise your hand for Alice." Not as many arms went into the air. "It looks like Tom is our winner."

Another groan, and she wagged her finger in mock sternness. "We voted fair and square. Besides, we'll read about Alice eventually. I will begin, then pass the book, and each of you will read a page."

"A whole page?" This from Harold Snyder. "That's a lot to read."

His bench buddy Milton Giles nudged Harold's shoulder. "If you're not careful, she'll make you read two for that crack."

"Tempting, Milton," Ivy said, "But I don't want any of you to see reading as a punishment. It's my hope that you'll get so caught up in the story you won't mind the effort to read." She sent the boys an encouraging smile, then walked around her desk and sat in the wooden Windsor-style chair. One of these days, she'd take an evening to make a cushion. "The book begins with a preface written by Mr. Twain. 'Most of the adventures in this book really occurred; one or two experiences of my own, the rest those of boys who were schoolmates of mine. Huck Finn is drawn from life; Tom Sawyer also, but not from an individual; he is a combination of three boys whom I knew, and therefore belongs to the composite order of architecture.'"

As she read, she peeked over the book at the students and stifled a smile. To a person, they were already engrossed in Mr. Twain's words. She finished the preface and moved on to the first chapter. Three pages later, she stood and handed the book to Minnie Whitfield. The little girl's voice was clear and sweet, and Ivy was soon as absorbed as the students. Time passed, and the book was handed from child to child.

Nearly a half hour had passed when Ivy rose from the desk. "Well done, children. We'll take a few minutes to let each of you share your favorite scene from the book, then we'll do some arithmetic. It's such a lovely day, we'll go outside for science." She waggled her eyebrows. "Perhaps even conduct an experiment or two."

Movement outside the window caught her eye, and she craned her neck to look through the glass, her heart pounding. Nothing, then a hat appeared at the next window, the tan hat of the ranch hand who'd been doing guard duty. Ivy rolled her eyes and willed her racing pulse to slow. She needed to stop jumping at shadows.

The morning progressed, and she soon moved the students outside, but it wasn't long before the prickling sensation on her neck returned. She feigned a calmness she didn't feel as she surreptitiously surveyed the area, focusing on the fields. No movement, no glint from field glasses. A gust of wind tugged at her bonnet, then the acrid smell of tobacco assailed her nose. She glanced at the ranch hand—what *was* his name—but he held no pipe or one of the nasty cigarettes that had become the rage. Was she imagining things?

The young man stiffened and turned toward the fields, staring for several minutes into the unharvested corn.

She wasn't imagining things. Gaping, she watched the cowboy mount his horse and gallop across the expanse. The stalks rustled as someone threaded his way through them. Then a dark figure appeared above the corn, mounted on a horse. Her guard stopped at the edge of the field and watched whomever it was disappear. A moment later, the young man wheeled his horse around and trotted back to the schoolyard. He doffed his hat. "I'm sorry to have missed him, but I didn't think Mr. Pendleton would want me tearing up a farmer's cornfield. I also didn't think he'd want me to leave you unattended."

A shudder slithered up Ivy's spine, and she nodded. Nathan had been right in his estimation of the danger. Whoever had been in that field was up to no good. Two days remained until the wedding, but she would dismiss the students immediately and cancel classes until she returned. She couldn't risk the children's safety, and she'd been arrogantly naïve to believe nothing would happen. Papa or the despicable Mr. Heisel would never give up until they found her, and the amount of money offered as reward ensured bounty hunters wouldn't either.

Wrapping her arms around her middle, she said, "Time is of the essence, sir. I'll send the children home, then we can visit the sheriff together before heading to the ranch to tell Nathan."

The young man's face flushed. "I'm not a 'sir,' Miss Cregg. Just Jake."

"Well, Jake, you must call me Ivy."

His eyes widened. "Oh, no, ma'am. Mr. Pendleton would have my hide, but I appreciate the offer. It's mighty nice of you." He clamped his hat on his head, then motioned to the wagon. "I'll hitch up your horse, then we'll see the little ones home before I escort you to Sheriff Denard."

"An excellent plan. I won't be but a few minutes." She raised her chin and tried to look more confident than she felt. Would they arrive at the sheriff's office unharmed?

Chapter Twenty-Three

Ivy ran the cloth over the nightstand in the room she'd been assigned in Slade's house. After yesterday's visit to the sheriff, Slade insisted she remain at his place until the wedding two days hence. Dinah was also staying in the house to keep wagging tongues at bay. The house was pristine, but Ivy had tired of reading, and she'd baked enough cookies to keep the hands in treats for a week. Dusting the handcrafted furniture, and exploring the nooks and crannies, helped her get to know her intended. There were very few knickknacks, but he was obviously a voracious reader with stacks of books scattered throughout the house, including his own bedside table.

Her cheeks warmed at the memory of opening the door to his bedroom and peeking inside. No one was around to scold her, but her mother would have been scandalized at her boldness. Curiosity had gotten the better of her, and she'd crept down the hall to see what the room said about him. With unadorned cherrywood furniture, navy-blue curtains and quilt, and nothing hanging on the dark blue walls, the room screamed masculinity. Would he allow her to change the décor? She heard a noise from below, so she'd shut the door and scurried to her room where she'd been ever since.

The situation was serious, but she'd still been surprised at the sheriff's stern reaction to her report. He'd commented more than once that he would ensure her safety and get rid of the "vermin" who thought he could show up in Lincoln and harm one of its citizens. Then after quizzing Jake and her for nearly thirty minutes, he'd ordered one of his deputies to escort them to Dinah's house where she'd packed her things and waited for Slade.

He'd nearly come out of his skin when he'd heard what happened, then he'd apologized multiple times for not being at the schoolyard. She'd assured him that Jake had handled the situation, but her fiancé did not appear convinced. That's when he'd insisted that she stay at his ranch, and Dinah agreed. Ivy wasn't sure if she felt cared for or stifled. Fortunately, her friend had given her space and was somewhere else in the house.

Finished cleaning, Ivy tossed the cloth in the hamper, then dropped into the burgundy brocade channel-back chair at the window and gazed outside. Like ants at a picnic, cowboys busied themselves with the myriad tasks associated with the ranch. Near the barn, two men were working with a large black horse who did not seem interested in cooperating. Slade had explained how a horse was broken, and that the process took as much as a month or six weeks depending on the animal's temperament. This giant beast would no doubt give the hands a run for their money.

Farther away, several hands were on horseback herding cattle from one pasture to another. Probably taking advantage of the beautiful day, two more cowboys were shoeing horses in front of the barn rather than inside. Her experience with horses was limited to the docile creatures that were hitched to wagons and carriages, and she'd never given a thought about what it took to feed, house, and care for them. How sheltered she'd been.

She pressed her hand against the glass, the warmth of the pane seeping into her palm. How life had changed in such a short time. Could she be the wife Slade needed her to be? A ranch wife? So very different from a city wife. Both he and Dinah had been patient in guiding her, but what if he woke up one day and realized he'd made a terrible decision in marrying a woman so unprepared? She'd brought nothing but danger to his life. Her hostessing, dancing, and needlepoint skills were of little use on the prairie. And yet, he'd agreed to marry her. In fact, he seemed eager to do so.

A sigh seeped out, and Ivy shook her head. She was getting maudlin. Pushing herself to her feet, she smoothed her skirts. Last night, Slade had taken her into his office and explained the financial side of the ranch, showing her where he kept his ledgers and files. He'd even given her the combination to the safe. A simple gesture, but one that brought tears to her eyes. He trusted her. She'd repay that trust by becoming so knowledgeable about running the books, she could free up some of his time. He worked hard. Too hard. He deserved time to enjoy the fruits of his labor.

The door swung open, and the new ranch hand stood on the threshold leering at her.

Ivy gulped, then raised her chin. "Mr. Hoyle! It is highly inappropriate for you to be here. You must leave immediately."

"Yeah, not going to happen." He strode into the room, grabbed her arm, and yanked her toward the corridor. "You and me are going for a little ride."

She opened her mouth to scream, and he raised his hand as if to slap her. She clamped her lips together but refused to cower, instead glaring at him with a set jaw.

Chuckling, he leaned close, his sour breath causing her stomach to flip. Opening his jacket, he revealed a pistol tucked into a worn leather holster. "I wouldn't do that if I was you. I haven't hurt anybody, but if you bring 'em runnin', I might just have to."

Nodding, she straightened her spine. "I'm assuming you're one of the many bounty hunters eager to make a quick buck by taking me home. You do realize Slade can match or beat whatever my father or his crony has promised you."

"Maybe, but it's too late now. I've got a reputation, you know. If I take money from the mark, no one will ever hire me again."

"Well, we wouldn't want to besmirch your precious reputation, would we?" Sarcasm colored Ivy's words. "You won't have to worry about that once Slade and his men stop you."

"Shut up," he growled. "We're gonna slip out through the kitchen where I've got a horse waiting." His gaze raked her from tip to toe. "And a hat and coat to hide the fact that you're a woman."

Shuddering, Ivy nearly swooned. Would he try to have his way with her? *Dear God, please keep me safe!*

"Get movin' or I'll toss you over my shoulder like a sack of potatoes. Daylight's burnin'."

He marched her down the stairs, through the corridor, and into the kitchen where Dinah was gagged and bound to a chair. Her eyes were wide, and a red outline of a hand marred her tear-streaked cheeks.

"You lied about not hurting anyone." Ivy tried to extricate herself from the man's grip. "Let me go."

"I lied about a lot of things, now keep movin.' She'll be fine." He tightened his grasp and pulled Ivy to the door. He twisted the knob and dragged her outside.

Ivy swallowed a sob. Where was the cowboy who was supposed to be watching the house? Had Mr. Hoyle hurt him, too. Or worse? How many more people would be harmed because of her?

Ivy's Inheritance

Chapter Twenty-Four

Whistles and shouts faded in the distance as Slade urged Midnight into a gallop. The hands were nearly finished for the day as the sun headed toward the horizon, and he desperately needed a bath before taking Ivy into town for dinner. She'd been a good sport about remaining in the house under the watchful eye of Dinah and Mrs. Ridings. He knew she'd much rather be surrounded by the children at school or working in the garden rather than trapped inside.

Purple and pink streaks appeared in the cloudless sky. He inhaled deeply the earthy aromas that filled the air. Moving to Nebraska had been the best decision of his life. He would never tire of the state's beauty, and God had blessed him beyond measure. And now, the Lord had sent him a wife, a woman who'd proved herself full of faith, integrity, and grace. She worried that she didn't have the skills of a prairie wife, but those could be taught.

Midnight's hooves thundered across the pastures, kicking up clods of dirt, and Slade gripped the reins. The massive, powerful animal was the fastest he'd ever owned, but the beast had the heart of a child, sweet and loving. They approached the barn, and Midnight snorted as Slade pulled back on the traces. "You do love to run, don't you, boy?" He patted the horse's neck before sliding to the ground, then led the animal into the barn.

Silence greeted him.

Where was Sandy? The lad should still be mucking out stalls. He was a dependable sort and wouldn't leave a job undone. Slade wrapped Midnight's reins on the iron hook, then strode through the vast building, peeking into stalls, the tack room, and the feed storage room. Nothing. Slade glanced at the hay loft. Surely, the boy hadn't decided on a nap. "Sandy?" He cocked his head as his voice echoed. Still nothing.

His gut tightened. Had something happened? He strode from the barn and looked toward the house. All seemed quiet and in order. Pursing his lips, he circled the barn but found no sign of the young hand. Slade jogged to the house and took the steps two at a time, then pushed open the door. "Ivy? Dinah?"

A thud sounded from the kitchen, and he ran down the corridor, boots thudding against the wooden floor. If nothing was wrong, Dinah would skin him alive for bringing dirt and manure inside. He crested the threshold and gasped, then rushed forward and dropped to his knees in front of Dinah, who was gagged and tied to one of the chairs. His heart beat wildly in his chest as he fumbled to untie the dirty cloth wrapped around her mouth. "Ivy. Where's Ivy?"

Dinah's face was soaked with tears, and her eyes were wide with fear. The beginning of a bruise was on her right cheek.

Nausea swept over him as he realized the ugly truth. "Ivy's gone, isn't she? She's been taken, hasn't she?" He finally managed to loosen the knot, and the gag fell away. "Where's Jake? He was supposed to be guarding the house. Tell me." He untied the ropes from around her arms and ankles.

She opened her mouth to speak but was overcome with coughing.

He climbed to his feet and grabbed a glass from the cabinet, then poured water from a pitcher into the vessel. He held the glass to her lips, and she sipped. Finally, she nodded and pushed away his hands.

"I'm sorry I couldn't keep her safe, Slade." Her chin trembled. "This is all my fault."

He stroked her head. "No, it's not, Dinah. Jake was on guard. You were simply here to keep her company. I know you're a strong woman, but you can't best an armed man when he takes you by surprise."

"How did you know?" Her voice cracked.

Slade forced a smile, but his pulse still raced. Time was burning, but going off half-cocked wouldn't do Ivy any good. "Because you would have bested him. Now, can you give me a description? I'm going to pull a few of the lads together and leave the rest here to run things while we follow the trail. I'll send Monty into town to tell the sheriff and collect more men. This mongrel will regret stealing Ivy, no matter how much reward money is on the table." He squatted in front of her again. "Can you give me a description? I don't suppose you happened to see his horse."

"Oh, Slade, you're going to be so angry." She gripped his hands. "It was Will Hoyle. He's a bounty hunter."

Biting back an oath, he stifled the desire to jump to his feet and punch a hole in the nearest wall. The act would frighten Dinah, create work for later, and not help the situation in any way. But it sure would feel good. *Lord, please keep Ivy safe and help me find her.* He met Dinah's tear-filled gaze. "Don't blame yourself. There was nothing you could have done. This is on me. I never should have left her alone. I should have been by her side every moment. And I *never* should have hired Hoyle."

Dinah squeezed his fingers. "He would have found a way, Slade." She released his hands. "Go find our girl, and I will pray like I've never prayed before. God will save her. Of that, I'm sure. He will guide you."

"I wish I had your faith."

"You do. It's just hard to find in awful times like this. But it's there." She pressed her hand against his chest. "Now, go. I'll be fine." Her green gaze held a glint of steel. "It's times like this I wish I were a man and could come with you. I owe that man a good working over."

"Dinah!" He gaped at her. "I've never—"

"Anger's the sin that gets me into trouble most often." She shrugged. "But I'll be praying about that, too. At some point I need to forgive him, and that's going to take a lot of doing."

"For me as well." He embraced her, then stroked her hair. "You're an amazing woman, Dinah Childs. Nathan is blessed to call you wife."

"Remind him of that when you see him." She shot him a tremulous smile, but he saw the strength underneath. She was trying to introduce some levity in the worst day of his life. "In your haste to leave don't forget to take some lanterns."

He climbed to his feet. "Do you feel up to pulling together some food for us while I go tell the lads what's happened? I'm hoping to be back in a day, but"—he swallowed against the lump that had formed in his throat—"that might not be the case."

"Absolutely." She rose with a wince, then straightened her spine. "And I'll grab a shawl and Ivy's coat. He dragged her out of here without one."

"Thank you." The words came out in a whisper. He couldn't think about Ivy cold and frightened, or he'd lose his focus, do something foolish that might endanger her. He'd rather find her and Hoyle before they boarded the train for Pennsylvania, but he'd follow her across the entire country if necessary. Might not be a bad thing if it gave him a chance to give her father a piece of his mind.

Shoving open the back door, he stepped outside. A few feet away, Jake lay crumpled on the ground, his complexion gray, and his eyes open and staring. A large gash marred his forehead. Slade heaved a loud sigh. Hoyle wasn't a bounty hunter. Bounty hunters didn't kill innocent men. He was a treasure hunter willing to do whatever necessary for the reward. Which meant Ivy was in more danger than he thought.

Chapter Twenty-Five

The acrid smell of sweat and manure assailed Ivy's nose as she clung to the saddle horn on the racing horse. Will held her tightly against his chest despite her efforts to separate herself from him. His rancid breath huffed in her ear. She pressed her lips together to keep from crying out as her body jerked with the motion of the animal whose hooves covered vast distances in a short time. The terrain changed to rolling hills, then higher peaks. Trees dotted the landscape, then became thicker.

Dropping toward the horizon, the sun would soon be gone, making it difficult for Slade to follow the trail. Would he be able to find her? Everyone knew Will would head to Pennsylvania to return her, but would he take the train or drag her across country on horseback and in carriages? He was not stupid. She'd seen intelligence in his dark gaze. But she'd also seen evil. *Please, God, save me!*

Should she try to escape? Or would that make things worse for her? If she faked a docile attitude, would he lower his guard, thus making it possible to get away?

Wait, My child.

Her head snapped up as her stomach hollowed. God was watching and held her in His hand. She'd tossed frantic prayers heavenward, but then was surprised when He responded. She nearly laughed out loud. What was the phrase from the Bible? Oh, ye of little faith. *Thank You, Father.*

Darkness fell, and her captor slowed the horse to a walk. They'd ridden for hours, and Ivy's muscles ached in protest. She shivered as the temperature dropped. Her wool coat was snugly hung in the chiffonade, and her thin dress did little to protect her from the elements. Will would be too smart to build a fire that could be seen.

He finally reined the horse to a stop a few yards from a wooded area. "Stay put, and don't do anything stupid," he said.

She gave him a curt nod. What would he think if she told him she was obeying God and not his command?

Hoyle slid to the ground, then led the horse into the forest, branches snapping under the animal's hooves. Bats chirped and squeaked overhead, and Ivy tightened her grip on the pommel and tried not to flinch. They were more interested in the mosquitos and other insects than in her, but she still didn't trust them not to swoop down at any moment.

When she thought she couldn't hold on for another second, they came to a large clearing and Will stopped the horse, then helped her off the animal. Her knees buckled, and she fell to the ground in a heap. He grabbed an arm and yanked her to her feet. "I said no funny business."

"Do you see me laughing?" She wrenched herself from his grasp and put out a hand to brace herself against one of the trees lest she pitch forward again. "For your information, I'm exhausted, and if you were any kind of a gentleman, you would know that. I'm not trying any funny business, as you call it. My muscles are sore and overused and can barely hold me, so I'll be sitting on a log somewhere while you set up camp. And I'd appreciate a fire. I'm cold, and the temperatures will only get colder as the night progresses."

He guffawed, the sound sending the bats higher into the sky. "Well, aren't you a pistol?" He removed his hat and bowed for a moment. "Is there anything else Your Highness would like besides a fire?"

"As a matter of fact, yes." She motioned to the horse. "I'd like the blanket."

Another disquieting laugh, then, "What will I do for warmth?"

"You are wearing a leather coat. I have nothing. You snatched me from my home without my coat." She fisted her hands on her hips. "Shame on you. And frankly, my father won't want me to arrive home in ill-health, so you may want to consider how you're going to take care of me until we get there."

She couldn't see his eyes in the darkness, but his stance changed. For the first time since he'd kidnapped her, he seemed uncertain.

"I have a plan. Don't you worry your pretty little head." He unbuckled the strap holding the blanket to the saddle, then tossed the aromatic wool at her. "Here. Now, sit down and be quiet. I've gotta take care of the horse and build the fire." He rummaged in the saddlebag, then handed her a cloth-wrapped package. "I'm not cookin' so that's your dinner. Save some for me."

Nodding, she trudged to the edge of the clearing and lowered herself on a fallen log, then wrapped the blanket around her shoulders. It smelled of sweat, but it kept the chill at bay, so she couldn't complain. Ivy unfolded the fabric to find a collection of what she could only assume was jerky. She bent and sniffed the dark, shriveled pieces of meat. A sharp, tangy smell that wasn't totally unpleasant wafted toward her. She picked up one of the chunks and tried to nibble off a bite. Too tough. Another attempt with no success.

"Good grief. Ya gotta tear it with your teeth." Will marched toward her and grabbed one of the pieces nestled in the bundle, then put the strip in the side of his mouth, bit down hard, and tore off a bite. "You'll starve to death at the rate you're going." Shaking his head, he shoved the jerky into the front pocket of his flannel shirt, then pivoted and stalked back to the horse.

Her face burned as she mimicked his motions with the jerky. Her stomach lurched as she chewed. And chewed. And chewed. Would this interminable journey never end?

Help me find her. Help me find her. Help me find her. Slade bent over Midnight's neck, his prayers matching the rhythm of the horse's pounding hooves. A half-dozen of his hands followed close behind. Before darkness had completely enveloped them, they'd found Hoyle's tracks and determined that he was headed into the mountains. There were two trails the man could take, and after a short discussion, the posse had decided to follow the easier of the two, figuring Hoyle wouldn't want to subject Ivy to the more difficult climb. To receive the reward, the man needed to get her home in good condition.

Ivy. An image of her beautiful face appeared in his head. Was she cold? Frightened? Of course, she was, but she was also a woman of faith. And tenacity. She might be out of her element, but she'd never show it. In fact, Hoyle might have to gag her to keep her quiet. Otherwise, she'd spend the trip giving him what for. Slade would laugh if he wasn't so worried. His precious Ivy was in the hands of a killer, and the only thing keeping her alive was the man's greed.

Slowing Midnight to a walk, Slade peered into the inky blackness. Why did tonight have to be a moonless night? A full moon would have lit their path like a lantern. He huffed out a sigh and cast an eye to the sky, the pinpoints of the constellations bright against the dark expanse. He nearly slapped himself. The constellations, of course! Sailors had been using them for centuries as a guide, and he could, too. He'd spent countless hours as a child looking at the sky, then during the endless nights after battle picking out the outlines of the mythical figures to the sound of men's moaning. Ironically, it was the stars that had kept him grounded in those dark moments when all seemed lost. He'd been reminded of God's sovereignty. God, Who'd placed every star and planet in the sky. When Slade has said as much to Ronnie, one of his platoon mates, the man had scoffed, claiming God was too big to be interested in anything humanity had managed to get themselves into. But Slade knew differently.

"Whoa." Slade reined Midnight to a stop, and his hands did the same, gathering around him in a tight circle. "I know you're exhausted, men, but the blackguard will stop for the night, which means we can catch up shortly before sunrise if we continue on. I'm hoping he thinks we won't try to find him in the darkness, and we'll have the element of surprise. Are you with me?"

Murmured assents peppered the air, and Slade's chest swelled. He couldn't ask for a better group of men. "Thank you." He motioned toward the sky. "Most of you have been riding for decades, so you may already know about the constellations, but I don't want any confusion, so I'm going to explain how they'll guide the way. I don't mean any disrespect to your knowledge or abilities."

"Anything to find Miss Ivy, boss," Monty said. "I don't know about the other boys, but I could use a primer myself."

Slade smiled. Good old Monty. Always making sure the lads felt comfortable. "All right." He spoke slowly, gesturing to the various star combinations as he explained the route and what he planned to do when they found Hoyle. Because they would find the culprit. Despite his fear for Ivy, in his heart, he knew God would lead him to where they were holed up. He didn't know how he knew, but he knew. Ivy would tell him that was his faith in action. There was one more thing he needed to do before they set off on the last leg of their journey. "Lads, I'd like to pray for us. I should have done so before we left the ranch, and I'm embarrassed I didn't think of it."

"You was worried, boss," Micah piped up. "It's understandable."

"Thanks, son, but when you're worried, that's the most important time." Slade pulled off his hat, cleared his throat, and bowed his head. A cool breeze stroked his cheek. "Dear Father, I'm not good at fancy prayers, and I'm trying to leave this whole situation in Your hands, but I'm struggling. I'm angry at Hoyle, angry at Ivy's papa for creating this whole mess, and angry at myself for not seeing who Hoyle is. Keep Ivy safe, Father. Grant her Your peace so she knows we're coming for her. Keep me and the lads safe, too. Prevent us from getting hurt or killed, and thank You for placing the stars in the sky to lead us. Amen."

A chorus of amens following, then rustling as the men donned their hats. Tack jingled as they moved into a line.

"Let's go get our gal, boss." Monty's voice floated toward him, then a chuckle from the rest of the men.

Slade's grin was more of a grimace, but he appreciated their attempt to lighten the mood. He spurred Midnight into a walk. Too fast, and the animal could stumble over a rock or divot and potentially break a leg. Minutes passed, then hours. Their steady pace had brought them to the wooded base of the mountain sooner than expected, and Slade sent up a grateful prayer.

In the distance, a light flickered, and he squinted to peer into the darkness. Were his eyes playing tricks on him, or was he really seeing the glow of a campfire? He held up his hand to stop the lads, and Monty whispered, "Not as smart as he thinks, boss, building a fire. He may as well be sitting in the middle of a pasture at noon."

"Indeed." Slade turned his horse to face the hands. "We'll ride up to the edge of the trees, then Monty and I will dismount and head in. The rest of you fellas will fan out and be ready if he tries to make a break for it." He unholstered his gun, praying he wouldn't need the weapon, but Hoyle had proven himself to be a killer, so Slade wouldn't take any chances.

Thirty minutes later, they arrived where the trees met the valley, and Slade slid from Midnight's back, then handed the reins to Micah. Beside him, Monty swung down to the ground and handed his reins to one of the other lads. He clapped Slade on the back in a quick show of solidarity and encouragement before turning his face toward the woods.

The two men crept forward following the firelight. A few yards from the clearing, they stopped and surveyed the situation. They'd arrived none too soon.

Hoyle was saddling the horse, and Ivy was huddled under a worn blanket near the fire. She alternately stared into the flames and glared at her captor. She appeared unharmed, and relief swept over Slade. He pointed to Ivy, then Monty, and the old hand nodded. Then Slade held up his hand, then mouthed the words as he lowered his fingers one by one in a silent countdown.

He tightened his grip on his Colt, then burst into the clearing. "Hands up, Hoyle."

Hoyle whirled and reached toward his hip but came up empty. His holster lay on the ground near his saddlebags. His shoulders sagged, and he raised his arms in surrender. He glared at Slade. "Captured by a fancy-pants limey and an old man. So much for my reputation."

Ivy leapt up, the blanket falling to the ground, and rushed toward Slade. He enveloped her in his arms as Monty laughed and walked toward the bounty hunter. "I'll be sure to spread that around. Now, put your hands behind your back, so I can truss you up for the ride back to Lincoln."

"I don't suppose you'd let me go if I promise to leave the state."

Monty snorted. "Not gonna happen. You've gotta answer for what you did to Jake."

Slade stroked Ivy's hair and gazed into her eyes in the growing light. A smudge of dirt marred her chin, and her hair was a tangled mess, but she'd never looked more beautiful to him. "Are you all right? I wasn't there to prevent this, and I'm sorry."

She snaked her arms around his neck, then raised her mouth toward his, stopping a hairbreadth away. "Hush. There's no need to apologize. I'm fine. Well, more than fine, actually." She shot him a saucy smile before closing the distance in a heart-searing kiss.

A few moments later, Monty cleared his throat. "I, um, hate to break up this happy reunion, but the boys'll be wondering what's happening, and if we wait too long, they might come charging in."

With a chuckle, Slade broke the kiss, then buffed his nose against Ivy's. "He's right. And if we dawdle too long, we'll be late for this afternoon's wedding." He sobered. "Unless you want to wait a couple of days. To rest up."

She giggled. "No, sir. We're getting married today. Once the paper is signed, Papa can't do anything about his deal with Mr. Heisel. But more importantly"—she snuggled closer—"I want to spend the rest of my life with you, and I want that to start as soon as possible. No more waiting."

"No more waiting." Slade grinned and took hold of the reins on Hoyle's horse with one hand while lacing his fingers with Ivy's as they followed Monty and his charge out of the woods.

Epilogue

Déjà vu.

Ivy sat on the padded seat in front of the mirror in her teal dress, and Dinah stood behind her, hairbrush in hand, intent upon piling Ivy's dark hair on top of her head. Ringlets framed her face.

The last twenty-four hours seemed like a dream. The terror of being kidnapped, the exhausting journey, and the unexpected rescue by Slade and his men. She'd ridden back to the ranch nestled in Slade's arms on Midnight, and he'd suggested they wait for her to recuperate before holding the wedding, but she refused to wait another day to marry.

When they reached the house, Dinah had two of the men fill the tub with steaming hot water, and Ivy scrubbed herself until her skin shone, then she'd tumbled into bed and slept for nearly four hours.

"It's not fair, you looking so beautiful after such an ordeal." Dinah spoke through the hairpins clamped between her lips as she winked at Ivy. "Slade's never going to let you out of his sight again."

"That's what I'm afraid of." Ivy nodded. "I understand his skittishness, but he's got a ranch to run, and besides, once we're married, Papa and Mr. Heisel have no further claim on me."

"You really think they can be trusted not to try anything?"

She met Dinah's gaze in the reflection. "No, and I've given this a lot of thought. After the wedding, I'm going to cable Papa and ask him to come to Lincoln, so he can meet Slade, and we can offer to pay off his debt to Mr. Heisel. Papa is a prideful man, and I don't know if he'll accept, but I want to make the effort. I want him to know I forgive him."

Dinah's eyes widened. "You've forgiven him? Already?"

Nodding, Ivy said, "God has forgiven me. I can do no less. I'm not saying it was easy, and I'm sure the anger at what he did will surface now and again, but I can't let it fester. And if I'm to have any sort of relationship with Papa, I need to do my part, too."

"You're a better woman than me." Dinah shook her head. "But enough seriousness. You're getting married in less than an hour. A few more pins, and you'll be ready."

Ivy turned her head one way, then the other. "There are plenty of pins, thank you very much. I don't believe my hair is going anywhere and will hold up to the stiffest of winds."

Giggling, Dinah set down the brush. "All right. I just want it to be perfect."

"It is." Ivy rose and picked up the russet-colored gown from the bed. "Now, it's your turn. Can't have my matron of honor walk down the aisle in her wrapper, lovely as it is."

"No, that wouldn't do."

Chattering like magpies, they had Dinah dressed in a few minutes, then she pinned her hair into a simple chignon. "Done, and none to soon." She peeked out the window and motioned to the carriage that had pulled up in front of the house. "Your carriage awaits, Cinderella."

Ivy pressed one hand against her middle and took a deep breath. This was really happening. She was getting married to a man who adored her and whom she couldn't imagine living without. Yet, such a short time had elapsed since her arrival. Only God could have worked such a miracle. "Does that make you my fairy godmother?"

They burst out laughing, then hurried from the room and down the stairs. Slade had spent the day at Dinah's house with Nathan, so there was no worry that he would see her before the ceremony. They climbed into the conveyance, and it lurched forward. Several minutes later, the vehicle rolled to a stop in front of the church where a crowd of people were making their way inside. Dinah laid one hand on Ivy's arm. "We'll wait until everyone has gone in."

Ivy's stomach buzzed as if a chipmunk was dancing a jig, and her mouth dried. She wanted this more than anything. Why was she so nervous?

Finally, the street emptied, and it was time. Dinah pushed open the door, and the sound of the piano wafted toward them. "That's our cue."

Climbing to the ground, they smoothed their skirts, then ascended the steps into the church. Ivy peeked into the sanctuary, and her jaw dropped. Someone, or perhaps many someones had filled the church with flowers, ribbon streamers, and tulle. Just for her. Her heart swelled, and tears filled her eyes. Standing next to the preacher and Nathan, Slade beamed at her, his brown hair slicked back, and his chocolate-brown eyes filled with love. Her pulse tripped at how handsome he looked.

Dinah walked down the aisle, then the congregation stood and turned toward Ivy as she glided toward her groom. The ceremony passed in a blur as she murmured her responses. Then it came time for the ring, a beautiful square-shaped emerald flanked by three smaller emeralds on each side. She looked up at Slade. "You remembered."

He grinned at her. "I remember everything you've told me."

"You may kiss your bride," intoned Pastor Youst.

"Gladly." Slade winked at her ask he lowered his mouth to hers.

Ivy melted in his arms. Who knew she'd have to travel twelve hundred miles to find home?

The End

What did you think of *Ivy's Inheritance*?

Thank you so much for purchasing *Ivy's Inheritance*. You could have selected any number of books to read, but you chose this book.

I hope it added encouragement and exhortation to your life. If so, it would be nice if you could share this book with your family and friends by posting to one or more of your favorite social media outlets.

If you enjoyed this book and found some benefit in reading it, I'd appreciate it if you could take some time to post a review on Amazon, Kobo, BN, Goodreads, BookBub or other book review site of your choice. Your feedback and support will help me to improve my writing craft for future projects and make this book even better.

Thank you again for your purchase.

Blessings,

Linda Shenton Matchett

Ivy's Inheritance

Read chapter one of *Dinah's Dilemma*; where it all began in Lincoln, Nebraska:

Nathan Childs raced across the field toward his daughter as she toddled with determination toward the fire. How had he managed to let Florence get so far from his side? The three-year-old was fearless, and he knew better than to give her too much freedom. He'd already prevented her from crawling under the fence into the horse pen and trying to climb one of the massive sugar maples that sheltered the food tables at the town's Memorial Day celebration.

Perspiration trickled down his spine, and his shirt clung to his back as the midday sun beat down on his head and glared into his eyes. The morning had dawned unseasonably warm, and the temperatures continued to rise. Summers in Nebraska were known as scorchers, but May was early to be fighting heat and humidity.

"Florence," he shouted as he ran to gain the child's attention, but his voice was swallowed up in the myriad conversations, music, and laughter of Lincoln's citizens. Nebraska's capital had exploded in population over the last eighteen months, and Burlington and River Railroad's first train was due at the end of June. Sure to bring even more people. Not what he'd envisioned when he moved West after Georgianna's death.

Finally, close enough to grab her, he scooped Florence into his arms and pressed her close to his chest, her small body warm and soft. "What were you thinking, baby girl? Fire is bad. You need to be more careful and stay near me."

Ivy's Inheritance

"No!" She arched her back and flailed her legs. "Fire is pretty, Daddy." Her face reddened, and she sobbed as if she'd lost her best friend. Tears dampened her cheeks, her blue eyes swimming.

His heart dropped. He hated when she cried. Her sobs made him feel as helpless as a newborn calf. He never knew what to do when she got like this. He hugged her closer and rubbed circles on her back in an effort to calm her.

"Sounds like someone's tired."

Nathan turned and nodded.

His best friend and the town sheriff, Alfred Denard, approached, a wide grin creasing his face below his black Stetson hat. "How about if you take a break and let Livvy watch her for a while. Looks like you both could use a change of scenery."

"Is it that obvious?"

Alfred chuckled as they headed for the cluster of women seated under the trees. Sometimes I think you'd rather face the Mes Gang or Farrington Brothers than a crying little girl."

Nathan shrugged. "At least when I was chasing outlaws as a Pinkerton, I'd been trained and knew what to expect. Raising Florence is another whole ball of wax. Every day is different, so something I learned yesterday, doesn't necessarily work today." He blew out a deep breath as

Florence quieted and tucked her thumb into her mouth. "I love her with my whole being, but maybe I should have let Georgianna's parents take her. I'm failing miserably."

"Do you think living with her grandparents is what's best for her?"

Nearing the blanket where Alfred's wife, Olivia, sat, Nathan paused and grimaced. "I don't know anymore. The thought of having to decide paralyzes me."

Livvy rose and held out her arms, her blonde hair swept into a tight bun at the base of her neck. She smiled, and her face glowed. "Are you going to let me spend time with your sweet little girl, Nathan? I've been aching to hold that child all day."

Florence chortled and reached for the buxom young woman.

Nathan transferred his daughter into her waiting embrace, and his arms felt bereft. He shoved his hands into his pockets.

"Can I keep her through dinner, Nathan?" Livvy poked Florence's belly then rubbed noses with the giggling youngster. "We'll have lots of fun together, won't we?"

"You sure that's not too much time, Livvy?"

She shook her head. "Not enough, if you ask me." She jerked her head toward the corrals. "You boys head over to the pens and enjoy yourselves. The roping competitions should be starting soon."

Alfred ran his finger along her jaw then kissed her cheek, a starry-eyed look on his face. Married for three years, he still mooned over his wife, like a besotted schoolboy. Livvy had come from Atlanta as his friend's mail-order bride. Claiming love at first sight, they'd married immediately. "You holler if you need help, honey."

"I'll be fine." She winked at her husband. "Now, scoot."

Nathan pressed his lips together as his heart tugged. It had been too long since anyone looked at him like Livvy gazed at Alfred, but he had enough going on without saddling himself with a wife. He turned toward the festivities. He couldn't ask for better friends than Alfred and Livvy. Two days after he'd arrived fifteen months ago, they'd shown up at his claim with food and friendship. Between the two of them, they'd arranged for some of the locals to transport his supplies from Omaha then pulled together a cadre of men to help build the house and barn. Livvy kept him fed when he didn't feel like eating in those early days of mourning after Georgianna's death. He'd figured moving to a new location would lessen the hollow feeling in his heart since she'd never lived in Nebraska, but his grief had followed him. A city girl born and bred, she would have hated life on the plains, but he still missed her presence. Especially in the small things. Rustling up a stack of pancakes or sitting on the front porch watching the sun dip behind the trees, talking about everything and nothing.

The first year in Lincoln had been difficult, but rewarding. The crop had been decent, and he'd put aside some money for the future. Maybe to purchase the adjoining plot. Too soon to do so, but the idea was tempting. This year's wheat had done well and would be ready to harvest in another couple of months.

A stiff gust kicked up dust from the animal enclosures and swirled above the beasts. The acrid smell of manure clung to the breeze as it lifted his hat. Would he ever get used to the constant wind?

"All right, gents, time to see who's the best roper in the Lincoln." Barnard Johnson, a cattle rancher who owned the largest spread outside of town, stood in the center of one of the corrals, thumbs tucked in the waistband of his denim pants. A pair of ivory-handled pistols, Colts, if Nathan wasn't mistaken, hung from an ornate holster around his substantial belly. His boots gleamed.

Alfred jabbed Nathan with a sharp elbow. "You should take a turn. Show up the rest of the boys."

"No, thanks. I want to make friends not enemies."

"This is just a friendly competition."

"I'll pass, but you should take a turn. Confirm why you're the best sheriff in Nebraska."

"Because I can lasso the outlaws?" Alfred's chuckle rumbled in his chest. "Think I'll pass, too."

"Hey, Nathan. Aren't you going to show off those muscles of yours?"

Nathan cringed at the sound of Katrina Wainwright's strident voice that could send dogs and bats running for cover. She'd made her intentions clear at Christmas that he was the man for her despite his protestations to the contrary. Not one to be put off easily, she turned up at his side every chance she got. He squared his shoulders and pivoted on his heel. Dipping his head in greeting, he forced a smile. "Good afternoon, Miss Wainwright. Are you enjoying today's event?"

Her giggle ended with a snort as she slapped his arm. "Katrina. How many times do I have to remind you to call me by my given name?"

"It wouldn't be proper, Miss Wainwright."

"We're not exactly in a Boston drawing room."

"True—"

"Hey, Katrina, watch this!" From inside the corral, one of Mr. Johnson's cowhands waved his hands over his head. She turned, and Nathan took the opportunity to escape. Alfred followed close behind him. They strode to the six-foot tables piled with platters of food, grabbed a couple of plates, and chose several delicious-looking items. Nathan frowned. "That was a close one, but I feel bad for sneaking away."

"Don't. You've made it clear you're not interested. And after the incident with Florence when she took the child from the church nursery without your permission, she ought to know you'll never trust her." Alfred held an oatmeal cookie up to his nose and took a deep breath. "I do love my wife's baking." He took a bite and grinned. Shoving the rest of the treat into his mouth, he clapped Nathan on the back as he finished chewing. "I know how you can get rid of her."

Nathan narrowed his eyes. "I'm afraid to ask."

"Don't be. I have the perfect solution. You need a substitute girlfriend, and I know where you can get one."

"No. Before you say anything else, the answer is no. I'm not going to apply for a mail-order bride." Tears pricked the backs of his eyes. "You and Livvy are very happy, but I'm not in the market for a wife, and I don't think I'll ever be." He swallowed against the lump that had formed in his throat.

"I understand your grief. Don't forget I lost my first wife six years ago. But you can find love again. Unfortunately, the ratio of women to men out here isn't good, and your choices in Lincoln are limited." He wiggled his eyebrows. "Unless, you'd like to reconsider Miss Wainwright."

"Absolutely not." Nathan shuddered. "Despite her outward beauty, she's deceitful, and I could never love a woman like that. Florence and I are doing just fine with the two of us."

"Are you so sure about that? Your little girl needs a mother. You're not being fair to Florence. Please think about contacting Milly Crenshaw at the Westward Home and Hearts Matrimonial Agency." He squeezed Nathan's shoulder. "Now, as much as I enjoy time with you, I'm going to sit with my beautiful wife."

Nathan watched him leave, a jaunty air in his step as he threaded his way through the crowd to Livvy. She beamed as he approached then blushed after he bent and whispered something in her ear. Was Alfred right? Could he find a woman he would love as he had Georgianna? He surveyed the townspeople, his gaze stopping to rest on Katrina. Full figured with a peaches-and-cream complexion, she had ebony-colored hair and deep-brown eyes. A gorgeous woman evidenced by the number of young men crowding around her like a flock of chicks. But he couldn't get past her subterfuge. Plain and simple, she'd lied then claimed the whole thing was a misunderstanding. Should he try to find an honest woman who would love Florence as her own? Did this Milly Crenshaw have the answer? Surely, anyone she sent couldn't be any worse than Katrina.

Acknowledgments

Although writing a book is a solitary task, it is not a solitary journey. There have been many who have helped and encouraged me along the way.

My parents, Richard and Jean Shenton, who presented me with my first writing tablet and encouraged me to capture my imagination with words. Thanks, Mom and Dad!

Scribes212 – my ACFW online critique group that got me started on this journey: Valerie Goree, Marcia Lahti, and the late Loretta Boyett (passed on to Glory, but never forgotten). Without your input, my writing would not be nearly as effective.

Eva Marie Everson – my mentor/instructor with Christian Writers' Guild. You took a timid, untrained student and turned her into a writer. Many thanks!

SincNE, and the folks who coordinate the Crimebake Writing Conference. I have attended many writing conferences, but without a doubt, Crimebake is one of the best. The workshops, seminars, panels, critiques, and every tiny aspect are well-executed, professional, and educational.

Special thanks to Hank Phillippi Ryan, Halle Ephron, and Roberta Isleib for your encouragement and spot-on critiques of my work.

Paula Proofreader (https://paulaproofreader.wixsite.com/home): I'm so glad I found you! My work is cleaner because of your eagle eye. Any mistakes are completely mine.

A heartfelt thank you to my brothers, Jack Shenton and Douglas Shenton, and my sister, Susan Shenton Greger for being enthusiastic cheerleaders during my writing journey. Your support means more than you'll know.

My husband, Wes, deserves special kudos for understanding my need to write. Thank you for creating my writing room – it's perfect, and I'm thankful for it every day. Thank you for your willingness to accept a house that's a bit cluttered, laundry that's not always done, and meals on the go. I love you.

And finally, to God be the glory. I thank Him for giving me the gift of writing and the inspiration to tell stories that shine the light on His goodness and mercy.

Ivy's Inheritance

Other Titles by this Author

Romance

Love's Harvest, Wartime Brides, Book 1

Love's Rescue, Wartime Brides, Book 2

Love's Belief, Wartime Brides, Book 3

Love's Allegiance, Wartime Brides, Book 4

Spies & Sweethearts, Sisters in Service, Book 1

The Mechanic & The MD, Sisters in Service, Book 2

The Widow & The War Correspondent, Sisters in Service, Book 3

Gold Rush Bride Hannah, Gold Rush Brides, Book 1

Gold Rush Bride Caroline, Gold Rush Brides, Book 2

Gold Rush Bride Tegan, Gold Rush Brides, Book 2

Dinah's Dilemma, Westward Home & Hearts Mail Order Brides

Rayne's Redemption, Westward Home & Hearts Mail Order Brides

Daria's Duke, Westward Home & Hearts Mail Order Brides

Ellie's Escape, Westward Home & Hearts Mail Order Brides

Beryl's Bounty Hunter, Westward Home & Hearts Mail Order Brides

Ivy's Inheritance

Vanessa's Replacement Valentine, Brides of Pelican Rapids
A Family for Hazel, Brides of Pelican Rapids

A Bride for Seamus, Proxy Bride Series
A Bride for Keegan, Proxy Bride Series

Estelle's Endeavor, Thanksgiving Books & Blessings Series, Collection 5
Francine's Foibles, Thanksgiving Books & Blessings Series, Collection 6

Dial V for Valentine, You're On the Air Series
Dial S for Second Chances, You're On the Air Series

Love at First Flight
Love Found in Sherwood Forest
On the Rails: A Harvey Girls Story
A Love Not Forgotten
A Doctor in the House
War's Unexpected Gift
Love and Chocolate

Mystery
Under Fire, Ruth Brown Mystery Series, Book 1
Under Cover, Ruth Brown Mystery Series, Book 2

Ivy's Inheritance

Under Ground, Ruth Brown Mystery Series, Book 3

Murder of Convenience, Women of Courage, Book 1
Murder at Madison Square Garden, Women of Courage, Book 2

Non-Fiction

WWII Word Find, Volume 1

Let's Connect!

www.LindaShentonMatchett.com

www.facebook.com/LindaShentonMatchettAuthor

www.pinterest.com/lindasmatchett

www.linkedin.com/in/authorlindamatchett

https://www.goodreads.com/author_linda_matchett

https://www.bookbub.com/authors/linda-shenton-matchett

Interested in more historical fiction?

Visit http://www.lindashentonmatchett.com/p/books.html

Ivy's Inheritance

www.ingramcontent.com/pod-product-compliance
Lightning Source LLC
LaVergne TN
LVHW041930070526
838199LV00051BA/2766